DOVER · THRIFT · EDITIONS

The Gambler

FYODOR DOSTOYEVSKY

DOVER PUBLICATIONS, INC.
New York

DOVER THRIFT EDITIONS

GENERAL EDITOR: STANLEY APPELBAUM
EDITOR OF THIS VOLUME: PHILIP SMITH

Copyright

Copyright © 1996 by Dover Publications, Inc.
All rights reserved under Pan American and International Copyright Conventions.

Bibliographical Note

This Dover edition, first published in 1996, is an unabridged, slightly corrected republication of the Constance Garnett translation of *The Gambler*, as originally published in the collection *The Gambler and Other Stories* (Volume IX of the series *The Novels of Fyodor Dostoevsky*) by The Macmillan Company, New York, 1917. A new introductory Note has been specially prepared for the present edition.

Library of Congress Cataloging-in-Publication Data

Dostoyevsky, Fyodor, 1821–1881.
   [Igrok. English]
   The gambler / Fyodor Dostoyevsky.
       p.   cm —(Dover thrift editions)
   Romanized record.
   ISBN 0-486-29081-6 (pbk.)
   I. Title.   II. Series.
PG3326.I4   1996
891.73'3 — dc20

                                              95-35852
                                             CIP

Manufactured in the United States of America
Dover Publications, Inc., 31 East 2nd Street, Mineola, N.Y. 11501

Note

The Gambler (1866) stands among the more significant shorter works of Russian writer Fyodor Dostoyevsky (1821–1881). In addition to its literary merits, this short novel boasts several important connections to its author's life and career: it was written quickly during the composition of *Crime and Punishment*, one of the greatest novels of all time; its writing was hastened by the hiring of a young stenographer, Anna Snitkina, who was to become Dostoyevsky's second wife; and it discusses with great insight the psychology of desperate gambling, a compulsion which brought its author to the brink of ruin.

For interested readers, Dostoyevsky's earlier *Notes from the Underground* (1864) is also available in the Dover Thrift Editions series (0-486-27053-X).

THE GAMBLER

A NOVEL

(From the diary of a young man)

CHAPTER I

AT LAST I have come back from my fortnight's absence. Our friends have already been two days in Roulettenburg. I imagined that they were expecting me with the greatest eagerness; I was mistaken, however. The General had an extremely independent air, he talked to me condescendingly and sent me away to his sister. I even fancied that the General was a little ashamed to look at me. Marya Filippovna was tremendously busy and scarcely spoke to me; she took the money, however, counted it, and listened to my whole report. They were expecting Mezentsov, the little Frenchman, and some Englishman; as usual, as soon as there was money there was a dinner-party; in the Moscow style. Polina Alexandrovna, seeing me, asked why I had been away so long, and without waiting for an answer went off somewhere. Of course, she did that on purpose. We must have an explanation, though. Things have accumulated.

They had assigned me a little room on the fourth storey of the hotel. They know here that I belong to the *General's suite*. It all looks as though they had managed to impress the people. The General is looked upon by every one here as a very rich Russian grandee. Even before dinner he commissioned me, among other things, to change two notes for a thousand francs each. I changed them at the office of the hotel. Now we shall be looked upon as millionaires for a whole week, at least. I wanted to take Misha and Nadya out for a walk, but on the stairs I was summoned back to the General; he had graciously bethought him to inquire where I was taking them. The man is absolutely unable to look me straight in the face; he would like to very much, but every time I meet his

1

eyes with an intent, that is, disrespectful air, he seems overcome with embarrassment. In very bombastic language, piling one sentence on another, and at last losing his thread altogether, he gave me to understand that I was to take the children for a walk in the park, as far as possible from the Casino. At last he lost his temper completely, and added sharply: "Or else maybe you'll be taking them into the gambling saloon. You must excuse me," he added, "but I know you are still rather thoughtless and capable, perhaps, of gambling. In any case, though, I am not your mentor and have no desire to be, yet I have the right, at any rate, to desire that you will not compromise me, so to speak . . ."

"But I have no money," I said calmly; "one must have it before one can lose it."

"You shall have it at once," answered the General, flushing a little; he rummaged in his bureau, looked up in an account book, and it turned out that he had a hundred and twenty roubles owing me.

"How are we to settle up?" he said. "We must change it into thalers. Come, take a hundred thalers — the rest, of course, won't be lost."

I took the money without a word.

"Please don't be offended by my words, you are so ready to take offence. . . . If I did make an observation, it was only, so to speak, by way of warning, and, of course, I have some right to do so. . . ."

On my way home before dinner, with the children, I met a perfect cavalcade. Our party had driven out to look at some ruin. Two magnificent carriages, superb horses! In one carriage was Mlle. Blanche with Marya Filippovna and Polina; the Frenchman, the Englishman and our General were on horseback. The passers-by stopped and stared; a sensation was created; but the General will have a bad time, all the same. I calculated that with the four thousand francs I had brought, added to what they had evidently managed to get hold of, they had now seven or eight thousand francs; but that is not enough for Mlle. Blanche.

Mlle. Blanche, too, is staying at the hotel with her mother; our Frenchman is somewhere in the house, too. The footman calls him "Monsieur le Comte." Mlle. Blanche's mother is called "Madame la Comtesse"; well, who knows, they may be Comte and Comtesse.

I felt sure that M. le Comte would not recognize me when we assembled at dinner. The General, of course, would not have thought of introducing us or even saying a word to him on my behalf; and M. le Comte has been in Russia himself, and knows what is called an *outchitel* is very small fry. He knows me very well, however. But I must confess I made my appearance at dinner unbidden; I fancy the General forgot to give orders, or else he would certainly have sent me to dine at the *table d'hôte*. I came of my own accord, so that the General looked at me with astonishment. Kind-hearted Marya Filippovna immediately made a place for me; but my meeting with Mr. Astley saved the situation, and I could not help seeming to belong to the party.

I met this strange Englishman for the first time in the train in Prussia, where we sat opposite to one another, when I was travelling to join the family; then I came across him as I was going into France, and then again in Switzerland: in the course of that fortnight twice—and now I suddenly met him in Roulettenburg. I never met a man so shy in my life. He is stupidly shy and, of course, is aware of it himself, for he is by no means stupid. He is very sweet and gentle, however. I drew him into talk at our first meeting in Prussia. He told me that he had been that summer at North Cape, and that he was very anxious to visit the fair at Nizhni Novogorod. I don't know how he made acquaintance with the General; I believe that he is hopelessly in love with Polina. When she came in he glowed like a sunset. He was very glad that I was sitting beside him at the table and seemed already to look upon me as his bosom friend.

At dinner the Frenchman gave himself airs in an extraordinary way; he was nonchalant and majestic with every one. In Moscow, I remember, he used to blow soap bubbles. He talked a great deal about finance and Russian politics. The General sometimes ventured to contradict, but discreetly, and only so far as he could without too great loss of dignity.

I was in a strange mood; of course, before we were half through dinner I had asked myself my usual invariable question: "Why I went on dancing attendance on this General, and had not left them long ago?" From time to time I glanced at Polina Alexandrovna. She took no notice of me whatever. It ended by my flying into a rage and making up my mind to be rude.

I began by suddenly, apropos of nothing, breaking in on the conversation in a loud voice. What I longed to do above all things was to be abusive to the Frenchman. I turned round to the General and very loudly and distinctly, I believe, interrupted him. I observed that this summer it was utterly impossible for a Russian to dine at *table d'hôte*. The General turned upon me an astonished stare.

"If you are a self-respecting man," I went on, "you will certainly be inviting abuse and must put up with affronts to your dignity. In Paris, on the Rhine, even in Switzerland, there are so many little Poles, and French people who sympathize with them, that there's no chance for a Russian to utter a word."

I spoke in French. The General looked at me in amazement. I don't know whether he was angry or simply astonished at my so forgetting myself.

"It seems some one gave you a lesson," said the Frenchman, carelessly and contemptuously.

"I had a row for the first time with a Pole in Paris," I answered; "then with a French officer who took the Pole's part. And then some of the French came over to my side, when I told them how I tried to spit in Monseigneur's coffee."

"Spit?" asked the General, with dignified perplexity, and he even looked about him aghast.

The Frenchman scanned me mistrustfully.

"Just so," I answered. "After feeling convinced for two whole days that I might have to pay a brief visit to Rome about our business, I went to the office of the Papal Embassy to get my passport *viséed*. There I was met by a little abbé, a dried up little man of about fifty, with a frost-bitten expression. After listening to me politely, but extremely drily, he asked me to wait a little. Though I was in a hurry, of course I sat down to wait, and took up *L'Opinion Nationale* and began reading a horrible abusive attack on Russia. Meanwhile, I heard some one in the next room ask to see Monseigneur; I saw my abbé bow to him. I addressed the same request to him again; he asked me to wait — more drily than ever. A little later some one else entered, a stranger, but on business, some Austrian; he was listened to and at once conducted upstairs. Then I felt very much vexed; I got up, went to the abbé and said resolutely, that as Monseigneur was receiving, he might settle my business, too. At once the abbé drew back in great surprise. It was beyond his comprehension that an insignificant Russian should dare to put himself on a level with Monseigneur's guests. As though delighted to have an opportunity of insulting me, he looked me up and down, and shouted in the most insolent tone: 'Can you really suppose that Monseigneur is going to leave his coffee on your account?' Then I shouted, too, but more loudly than he: 'Let me tell you I'm ready to spit in your Monseigneur's coffee! If you don't finish with my passport this minute, I'll go to him in person.'

" 'What! When the Cardinal is sitting with him!' cried the abbé, recoiling from me with horror, and, flinging wide his arms, he stood like a cross, with an air of being ready to die rather than let me pass.

"Then I answered him that 'I was a heretic and a barbarian, *que je suis hérétique et barbare*,' and that I cared nothing for all these Archbishops, Cardinals, Monseigneurs and all of them. In short, I showed I was not going to give way. The abbé looked at me with uneasy ill-humour, then snatched my passport and carried it upstairs. A minute later it had been *viséed*. Here, wouldn't you like to see it?" I took out the passport and showed the Roman *visé*.

"Well, I must say . . ." the General began.

"What saved you was saying that you were a heretic and barbarian," the Frenchman observed, with a smile. "*Cela n'était pas si bête*."

"Why, am I to model myself upon our Russians here? They sit, not daring to open their lips, and almost ready to deny they are Russians. In Paris, anyway in my hotel, they began to treat me much more attentively when I told every one about my passage-at-arms with the abbé. The fat Polish *pan*, the person most antagonistic to me at *table d'hôte*, sank into the background. The Frenchmen did not even resent it when I told them that I had, two years previously, seen a man at whom, in 1812, a French *chasseur* had shot simply in order to discharge his gun. The man was at that time a child of ten, and his family had not succeeded in leaving Moscow."

"That's impossible," the Frenchman boiled up; "a French soldier would not fire at a child!"

"Yet it happened," I answered. "I was told it by a most respectable captain on the retired list, and I saw the scar on his cheek from the bullet myself."

The Frenchman began talking rapidly and at great length. The General began to support him, but I recommended him to read, for instance, passages in the "Notes" of General Perovsky, who was a prisoner in the hands of the French in 1812. At last Marya Filippovna began talking of something else to change the conversation. The General was very much displeased with me, for the Frenchman and I had almost begun shouting at one another. But I fancy my dispute with the Frenchman pleased Mr. Astley very much. Getting up from the table, he asked me to have a glass of wine with him.

In the evening I duly succeeded in getting a quarter of an hour's talk with Polina Alexandrovna. Our conversation took place when we were all out for a walk. We all went into the park by the Casino. Polina sat down on a seat facing the fountain, and let Nadenka play with some children not far from her. I, too, let Misha run off to the fountain, and we were at last left alone.

We began, of course, at first with business. Polina simply flew into a rage when I gave her only seven hundred guldens. She had reckoned positively on my pawning her diamonds in Paris for two thousand guldens, if not more.

"I must have money, come what may," she said. "I must get it or I am lost."

I began asking her what had happened during my absence.

"Nothing, but the arrival of two pieces of news from Petersburg: first that Granny was very ill, and then, two days later, that she seemed to be dying. The news came from Timofey Petrovitch," added Polina, "and he's a trustworthy man. We are expecting every day to hear news of the end."

"So you are all in suspense here?" I asked.

"Of course, all of us, and all the time; we've been hoping for nothing else for the last six months."

"And are *you* hoping for it?" I asked.

"Why, I'm no relation. I am only the General's step-daughter. But I am sure she will remember me in her will."

"I fancy you'll get a great deal," I said emphatically.

"Yes, she was fond of me; but what makes *you* think so?"

"Tell me," I answered with a question, "our *marquis* is initiated into all our secrets, it seems?"

"But why are you interested in that?" asked Polina, looking at me drily and austerely.

"I should think so; if I'm not mistaken, the General has already succeeded in borrowing from him."

"You guess very correctly."

"Well, would he have lent the money if he had not known about your 'granny'? Did you notice at dinner, three times speaking of her, he called her 'granny.' What intimate and friendly relations!"

"Yes, you are right. As soon as he knows that I have come into something by the will, he will pay his addresses to me at once. That is what you wanted to know, was it?"

"He will only begin to pay you his addresses? I thought he had been doing that a long time."

"You know perfectly well that he hasn't!" Polina said, with anger. "Where did you meet that Englishman?" she added, after a minute's silence.

"I knew you would ask about him directly."

I told her of my previous meetings with Mr. Astley on my journey.

"He is shy and given to falling in love, and, of course, he's fallen in love with you already."

"Yes, he's in love with me," answered Polina.

"And, of course, he's ten times as rich as the Frenchman. Why, is it certain that the Frenchman has anything? Isn't that open to doubt?"

"No, it is not. He has a chateau of some sort. The General has spoken of that positively. Well, are you satisfied?"

"If I were in your place I should certainly marry the Englishman."

"Why?" asked Polina.

"The Frenchman is better looking, but he is nastier; and the Englishman, besides being honest, is ten times as rich," I snapped out.

"Yes, but on the other hand, the Frenchman is a *marquis* and clever," she answered, in the most composed manner.

"But is it true?" I went on, in the same way.

"It certainly is."

Polina greatly disliked my questions, and I saw that she was trying to make me angry by her tone and the strangeness of her answers. I said as much to her at once.

"Well, it really amuses me to see you in such a rage. You must pay for the very fact of my allowing you to ask such questions and make such suppositions."

"I certainly consider myself entitled to ask you any sort of question," I answered calmly, "just because I am prepared to pay any price you like for it, and I set no value at all on my life now."

Polina laughed.

"You told me last time at the Schlangenberg, that you were prepared, at a word from me, to throw yourself head foremost from the rock, and it is a thousand feet high, I believe. I shall one day utter that word, solely in order to see how you will pay the price, and trust me I won't give way. You are hateful to me, just because I've allowed you to take such liberties, and even more hateful because you are so necessary to me. But so long as you are necessary to me, I must take care of you."

She began getting up. She spoke with irritation. Of late she had always ended every conversation with me in anger and irritation, real anger.

"Allow me to ask you, what about Mlle. Blanche?" I asked, not liking to let her go without explanation.

"You know all about Mlle. Blanche. Nothing more has happened since. Mlle. Blanche will, no doubt, be Madame la Générale, that is, if the rumour of Granny's death is confirmed, of course, for Mlle. Blanche and her mother and her cousin twice removed, the Marquis — all know very well that we are ruined."

"And is the General hopelessly in love?"

"That's not the point now. Listen and remember: take these seven hundred florins and go and play. Win me as much as you can at roulette; I must have money now, come what may."

Saying this, she called Nadenka and went into the Casino, where she joined the rest of the party. I turned into the first path to the left, wondering and reflecting. I felt as though I had had a blow on the head after the command to go and play roulette. Strange to say, I had plenty to think about, but I was completely absorbed in analysing the essential nature of my feeling towards Polina. It was true I had been more at ease during that fortnight's absence than I was now on the day of my return, though on the journey I had been as melancholy and restless as a madman, and at moments had even seen her in my dreams. Once, waking up in the train (in Switzerland), I began talking aloud, I believe, with Polina, which amused all the passengers in the carriage with me. And once more now I asked myself the question: "Do I love her?" And again I could not answer it, or, rather, I answered for the hundredth time that I hated her. Yes, she was hateful to me. There were moments (on every occasion at the end of our talks) when I would have given my life to strangle her! I swear if it had been possible on the spot to plunge a sharp knife in her bosom, I believe I should have snatched it up with relish. And yet I swear by all that's sacred that if at the Schlangenberg, at the fashionable peak, she really had said to me, "Throw yourself down," I should have thrown myself down at once, also with positive relish. I knew that. In one way or another it must be settled. All this she understood wonderfully well, and the idea that I knew, positively and distinctly, how utterly beyond my reach she was, how utterly impossible my mad dreams were of fulfilment, that thought, I am convinced, afforded her extraordinary satisfaction; if not, how could she, cautious and intelligent as she was, have been on such intimate and open terms with me? I believe she had hitherto looked on me as that empress of ancient times looked on the slave before whom she did not mind undressing because she did not regard him as a human being. Yes, often she did not regard me as a human being!

I had her commission, however, to win at roulette, at all costs. I had no time to consider why must I play, and why such haste, and what new scheme was hatching in that ever-calculating brain. Moreover, it was evident that during that fortnight new facts had arisen of which I had no idea yet. I must discover all that and get to the bottom of it and as quickly as possible. But there was no time now; I must go to roulette.

CHAPTER II

I CONFESS IT was disagreeable to me. Though I had made up my mind that I would play, I had not proposed to play for other people. It rather threw me out of my reckoning, and I went into the gambling saloon with very disagreeable feelings. From the first glance I disliked everything in it. I cannot endure the flunkeyishness of the newspapers of the whole world, and especially our Russian papers, in which, almost every spring, the journalists write articles upon two things: first, on the extraordinary magnificence and luxury of the gambling saloons on the Rhine, and secondly, on the heaps of gold which are said to lie on the tables. They are not paid for it; it is simply done from disinterested obsequiousness. There was no sort of magnificence in these trashy rooms, and not only were there no piles of gold lying on the table, but there was hardly any gold at all. No doubt some time, in the course of the season, some eccentric person, either an Englishman or an Asiatic of some sort, a Turk, perhaps (as it was that summer), would suddenly turn up and lose or win immense sums; all the others play for paltry guldens, and on an average there is very little money lying on the tables.

As soon as I went into the gambling saloon (for the first time in my life), I could not for some time make up my mind to play. There was a crush besides. If I had been alone, even then, I believe, I should soon have gone away and not have begun playing. I confess my heart was beating and I was not cool. I knew for certain, and had made up my mind long before, that I should not leave Roulettenburg unchanged, that some radical and fundamental change would take place in my destiny; so it must be and so it would be. Ridiculous as it may be that I should expect so much for myself from roulette, yet I consider even more ridiculous the conventional opinion accepted by all that it is stupid and absurd to expect anything from gambling. And why should gambling be worse than any other means of making money — for instance, commerce? It is true that only one out of a hundred wins, but what is that to me?

In any case I determined to look about me first and not to begin anything in earnest that evening. If anything did happen that evening it would happen by chance and be something slight, and I staked my money accordingly. Besides, I had to study the game; for, in spite of the thousand descriptions of roulette which I had read so eagerly, I understood absolutely nothing of its working, until I saw it myself.

In the first place it all struck me as so dirty, somehow, morally horrid and dirty. I am not speaking at all of the greedy, uneasy faces which by dozens, even by hundreds, crowd round the gambling tables. I see absolutely nothing dirty in the wish to win as quickly and as much as possible. I always thought very stupid the answer of that fat and prosperous moralist, who replied to some one's excuse "that he played for a very small stake," "So much the worse, it is such petty covetousness." As though covetousness were not exactly the same, whether on a big scale or a petty one. It is a matter of proportion. What is paltry to Rothschild is wealth to me, and as for profits and winnings, people, not only at roulette, but everywhere, do nothing but try to gain or squeeze something out of one another. Whether profits or gains are nasty is a different question. But I am not solving that question here. Since I was myself possessed by an intense desire of winning, I felt as I went into the hall all this covetousness, and all this covetous filth if you like, in a sense congenial and convenient. It is most charming when people do not stand on ceremony with one another, but act openly and aboveboard.

And, indeed, why deceive oneself? Gambling is a most foolish and imprudent pursuit! What was particularly ugly at first sight, in all the rabble round the roulette table, was the respect they paid to that pursuit, the solemnity and even reverence with which they all crowded round the tables. That is why a sharp distinction is drawn here between the kind of game that is *mauvais genre* and the kind that is permissible to well-bred people. There are two sorts of gambling: one the gentlemanly sort: the other the plebeian, mercenary sort, the game played by all sorts of riff-raff. The distinction is sternly observed here, and how contemptible this distinction really is! A gentleman may stake, for instance, five or ten louis d'or, rarely more; he may, however, stake as much as a thousand francs if he is very rich; but only for the sake of the play, simply for amusement, that is, simply to look on at the process of winning or of losing, but must on no account display an interest in winning. If he wins, he may laugh aloud, for instance; may make a remark to one of the bystanders; he may even put down another stake, and may even double it, but solely from curiosity, for the sake of watching and calculating the chances, and not from the plebeián desire to win. In fact, he must look on all gambling, roulette, *trente et quarante*, as nothing else than a pastime got up entirely for his amusement. He must not even suspect the greed for gain and the shifty dodges on which the bank depends. It would be extremely good form, too, if he should imagine that all the other gamblers, all the rabble, trembling over a gulden, were rich men and gentlemen like himself and were playing simply for their diversion and amusement. This complete ignorance of reality and innocent view of people would be, of course, extremely aristocratic. I have seen many mammas push forward their daughters, innocent and elegant Misses of fifteen and sixteen, and, giving them some gold coins, teach them how to play. The young lady wins or loses, invariably smiles and walks away, very well satisfied. Our General went up to the table with solid dignity; a flunkey rushed to hand him a chair, but he ignored the flunkey; he, very slowly and deliberately, took out his purse, very slowly and deliberately took three hundred francs in gold from his purse, staked them on the black, and won. He did not pick up his winnings, but left them on the table. Black turned up again; he didn't pick up his winnings that time either; and when, the third time, red turned up, he lost at once twelve hundred francs. He walked away with a smile and kept up his dignity. I am positive he was raging inwardly, and if the stake had been two or three times as much he would not have kept up his dignity but would have betrayed his feelings. A Frenchman did, however, before my eyes, win and lose as much as thirty thousand francs with perfect gaiety and no sign of emotion. A real gentleman should not show excitement even if he loses his whole fortune. Money ought to be so much below his gentlemanly dignity as to be scarcely worth noticing. Of course, it would have been extremely aristocratic not to notice the sordidness of all the rabble and all the surroundings. Sometimes, however, the opposite pose is no less aristocratic — to notice — that is, to look about one, even, perhaps, to stare through a lorgnette at the rabble; though always taking the rabble and the sordidness as nothing else but a diversion of a sort, as though it were a performance got up for the amusement of gentlemen. One may be jostled in that crowd, but one must look about one with complete conviction that one is oneself a spectator and that one is in no sense part of it. Though, again, to look very attentively is not quite the thing; that, again, would not be gentlemanly because, in any case, the spectacle does not deserve much, or close, attention. And, in fact, few spectacles do deserve a gentleman's close attention. And yet it seemed to me that all this was deserving of very close attention, especially for one who had come not only to observe it, but sincerely and genuinely reckoned himself as one of the rabble. As for my hidden moral convictions, there is no place for them, of course, in my present reasonings. Let that be enough for the present. I speak to relieve my conscience. But I notice one thing: that of late it has become horribly repugnant to me to test my thoughts and actions by any moral standard whatever. I was guided by something different . . .

The rabble certainly did play very sordidly. I am ready to believe, indeed, that a great deal of the most ordinary thieving goes on at the gambling table. The croupiers who sit at each end of the table look at the stakes and reckon the winnings; they have a great deal to do. They are rabble, too! For the most part they are French. However, I was watching and observing, not with the object of describing roulette. I kept a sharp look-out for my own sake, so that I might know how to behave in the future. I noticed, for instance, that nothing was more common than for some one to stretch out his hand and snatch what one had won. A dispute would begin, often an uproar, and a nice job one would have to find witnesses and to prove that it was one's stake!

At first it was all an inexplicable puzzle to me. All I could guess and distinguish was that the stakes were on the numbers, on odd and even, and on the colours. I made up my mind to risk a hundred guldens of Polina Alexandrovna's money. The thought that I was not playing for myself seemed to throw me out of my reckoning. It was an extremely unpleasant feeling, and I wanted to be rid of it as soon as possible. I kept feeling that by beginning for Polina I should break my own luck. Is it impossible to approach the gambling table without becoming infected with superstition? I began by taking out five friedrichs d'or (fifty gulden) and putting them on the even. The wheel went round and thirteen turned up—I had lost. With a sickly feeling I staked another five friedrichs d'or on red, simply in order to settle the matter and go away. Red turned up. I staked all the ten friedrichs d'or—red turned up again. I staked all the money again on the same, and again red turned up. On receiving forty friedrichs d'or I staked twenty upon the twelve middle figures, not knowing what would come of it. I was paid three times my stake. In this way from ten friedrichs d'or I had all at once eighty. I was overcome by a strange, unusual feeling which was so unbearable that I made up my mind to go away. It seemed to me that I should not have been playing at all like that if I had been playing for myself. I staked the whole eighty friedrichs d'or, however, on even. This time four turned up; another eighty friedrichs d'or was poured out to me, and, gathering up the whole heap of a hundred and sixty friedrichs d'or, I set off to find Polina Alexandrovna.

They were all walking somewhere in the park and I only succeeded in seeing her after supper. This time the Frenchman was not of the party, and the General unbosomed himself. Among other things he thought fit to observe to me that he would not wish to see me at the gambling tables. It seemed to him that it would compromise him if I were to lose too much: "But even if you were to win a very large sum I should be compromised, too," he added significantly. "Of course, I have no right to dictate your actions, but you must admit yourself . . ." At this point he broke off, as his habit was. I answered, drily, that I had very little money, and so I could not lose very conspicuously, even if I did play. Going upstairs to my room I succeeded in handing Polina her winnings, and told her that I would not play for her another time.

"Why not?" she asked, in a tremor.

"Because I want to play on my own account," I answered, looking at her with surprise; "and it hinders me."

"Then you still continue in your conviction that roulette is your only escape and salvation?" she asked ironically.

I answered very earnestly, that I did; that as for my confidence that I should win, it might be absurd; I was ready to admit it, but that I wanted to be let alone.

Polina Alexandrovna began insisting I should go halves with her in to-day's winnings, and was giving me eighty friedrichs d'or, suggesting that I should go on playing on those terms. I refused the half, positively and finally, and told her that I could not play for other people, not because I didn't want to, but because I should certainly lose.

"Yet I, too," she said, pondering, "stupid as it seems, am building all my hopes on roulette. And so you must go on playing, sharing with me, and—of course—you will."

At this point she walked away, without listening to further objections.

CHAPTER III

YET ALL YESTERDAY she did not say a single word to me about playing, and avoided speaking to me altogether. Her manner to me remained unchanged: the same absolute carelessness on meeting me; there was even a shade of contempt and dislike. Altogether she did not care to conceal her aversion; I noticed that. In spite of that she did not conceal from me, either, that I was in some way necessary to her and that she was keeping me for some purpose. A strange relation had grown up between us, incomprehensible to me in many ways when I considered her pride and haughtiness with every one. She knew, for instance, that I loved her madly, even allowed me to speak of my passion; and, of course, she could not have shown greater contempt for me than by allowing me to speak of my passion without hindrance or restriction. It was as much as to say that she thought so little of my feelings that she did not care in the least what I talked about to her and what I felt for her. She had talked a great deal about her own affairs before, but had never been completely open. What is more, there was this peculiar refinement in her contempt for me: she would know, for instance, that I was aware of some circumstance in her life, or knew of some matter that greatly concerned her, or she would tell me herself something of her circumstances, if to forward her objects she had to make use of me in some way, as a slave or an errand-boy; but she would always tell me only so much as a man employed on her errands need know, and if I did not know the whole chain of events, if she saw herself how worried and anxious I was over her worries and anxieties, she never deigned to comfort me by giving me her full confidence as a friend; though she often made use of me for commissions that were not only troublesome, but dangerous, so that to my thinking she was bound to be open with me. Was it worth her while, indeed, to trouble herself about my feelings, about my being worried, and perhaps three times as much worried and tormented by her anxieties and failures as she was herself?

I knew of her intention to play roulette three weeks before. She had even warned me that I should have to play for her, and it would be improper for her to play herself. From the tone of her words, I noticed even then that she had serious anxieties, and was not actuated simply by a desire for money. What is money to her for its own sake? She must have some object, there must be some circumstance at which I can only guess, but of which so far I have no knowledge. Of course, the humiliation and the slavery in which she held me might have made it possible for me (it often does) to question her coarsely and bluntly. Seeing that in her eyes I was a slave and utterly insignificant, there was nothing for her to be offended at in my coarse curiosity. But the fact is, that though she allowed me to ask questions, she did not answer them, and sometimes did not notice them at all. That was the position between us.

A great deal was said yesterday about a telegram which had been sent off four days before, and to which no answer had been received. The General was evidently upset and preoccupied. It was, of course, something to do with Granny. The Frenchman was troubled, too. Yesterday, for instance, after dinner, they had a long, serious talk. The Frenchman's tone to all of us was unusually high and mighty, quite in the spirit of the saying: "Sit a pig at table and it will put its feet on it." Even with Polina he was casual to the point of rudeness; at the same time he gladly took part in the walks in the public gardens and in the rides and drives into the country. I had long known some of the circumstances that bound the Frenchman to the General: they had made plans for establishing a factory together in Russia; I don't know whether their project had fallen through, or whether it was being discussed. Moreover, I had by chance come to know part of a family secret. The Frenchman had actually, in the previous year, come to the General's rescue, and had given him thirty thousand roubles to make up a deficit of Government monies missing when he resigned his duties. And, of course, the General is in his grip; but now the principal person in the whole business is Mlle. Blanche; about that I am sure I'm not mistaken.

What is Mlle. Blanche? Here among us it is said that she is a distinguished Frenchwoman, with a colossal fortune and a mother accompanying her. It is known, too, that she is some sort of relation of our marquis, but a very distant one: a cousin, or something of the sort. I am told that before I went to Paris, the Frenchman and Mlle. Blanche were on much more ceremonious, were, so to speak, on a more delicate and refined footing; now their acquaintance, their friendship and relationship, was of a rather coarse and more intimate character. Perhaps our prospects seemed to them so poor that they did not think it very necessary to stand on ceremony and keep up appearances with us. I noticed even the day before yesterday how Mr. Astley looked at Mlle. Blanche and her mother. It seemed to me that he knew them. It even seemed to me that our Frenchman had met Mr. Astley before. Mr. Astley, however, is so shy, so reserved and silent, that one can be almost certain of him—he won't wash dirty linen in public. Anyway, the Frenchman barely bows to him and scarcely looks at him, so he is not afraid of him. One can understand that, perhaps, but why does Mlle. Blanche not look at him either? Especially when the Marquis let slip yesterday in the course of conversation—I don't remember in what connection—that Mr. Astley had a colossal fortune and that he—the

Marquis — knew this for a fact; at that point Mlle. Blanche might well have looked at Mr. Astley. Altogether the General was uneasy. One can understand what a telegram announcing his aunt's death would mean!

Though I felt sure Polina was, apparently for some object, avoiding a conversation with me, I assumed a cold and indifferent air: I kept thinking that before long she would come to me of herself. But both to-day and yesterday I concentrated my attention principally on Mlle. Blanche. Poor General! He is completely done for! To fall in love at fifty-five with such a violent passion is a calamity, of course! When one takes into consideration the fact that he is a widower, his children, the ruin of his estate, his debts, and, finally, the woman it is his lot to fall in love with. Mlle. Blanche is handsome. But I don't know if I shall be understood if I say that she has a face of the type of which one might feel frightened. I, anyway, have always been afraid of women of that sort. She is probably five-and-twenty. She is well grown and broad, with sloping shoulders; she has a magnificent throat and bosom; her complexion is swarthy yellow. Her hair is as black as Indian ink, and she has a tremendous lot of it, enough to make two ordinary coiffures. Her eyes are black with yellowish whites; she has an insolent look in her eyes; her teeth are very white; her lips are always painted; she smells of musk. She dresses effectively, richly and with *chic*, but with much taste. Her hands and feet are exquisite. Her voice is a husky contralto. Sometimes she laughs, showing all her teeth, but her usual expression is a silent and impudent stare — before Polina and Marya Filippovna, anyway (there is a strange rumour that Marya Filippovna is going back to Russia). I fancy that Mlle. Blanche has had no sort of education. Possibly she is not even intelligent; but, on the other hand, she is striking and she is artful. I fancy her life has not passed without adventures. If one is to tell the whole truth, it is quite possible that the Marquis is no relation of hers at all, and that her mother is not her mother. But there is evidence that in Berlin, where we went with them, her mother and she had some decent acquaintances. As for the Marquis himself, though I still doubt his being a marquis, yet the fact that he is received in decent society — among Russians, for instance, in Moscow, and in some places in Germany — is not open to doubt. I don't know what he is in France. They say he has a chateau.

I thought that a great deal would have happened during this fortnight, and yet I don't know if anything decisive has been said between Mlle. Blanche and the General. Everything depends on our fortune, however; that is, whether the General can show them plenty of money. If, for instance, news were to come that Granny were not dead, I am convinced that Mlle. Blanche would vanish at once. It surprises and amuses

me to see what a gossip I've become. Oh! how I loathe it all! How
delighted I should be to drop it all, and them all! But can I leave Polina,
can I give up spying round her? Spying, of course, is low, but what do I
care about that?

I was interested in Mr. Astley, too, to-day and yesterday. Yes, I am
convinced he's in love with Polina. It is curious and absurd how much
may be expressed by the eyes of a modest and painfully chaste man,
moved by love, at the very time when the man would gladly sink into the
earth rather than express or betray anything by word or glance. Mr.
Astley very often meets us on our walks. He takes off his hat and passes
by, though, of course, he is dying to join us. If he is invited to do so, he
immediately refuses. At places where we rest — at the Casino, by the
bandstand, or before the fountain — he always stands somewhere not far
from our seat; and wherever we may be — in the park, in the wood, or on
the Schlangenberg — one has only to glance round, to look about one,
and somewhere, either in the nearest path or behind the bushes, Mr.
Astley's head appears. I fancy he is looking for an opportunity to have a
conversation with me apart. This morning we met and exchanged a
couple of words. He sometimes speaks very abruptly. Without saying
"good-morning," he began by blurting out —

"Oh, Mlle. Blanche! . . . I have seen a great many women like Mlle.
Blanche!"

He paused, looking at me significantly. What he meant to say by that I
don't know. For on my asking what he meant, he shook his head with a
sly smile, and added, "Oh, well, that's how it is. Is Mlle. Pauline very
fond of flowers?"

"I don't know; I don't know at all," I answered.

"What? You don't even know that!" he cried, with the utmost amazement.

"I don't know; I haven't noticed at all," I repeated, laughing.

"H'm! That gives me a queer idea."

Then he shook his head and walked away. He looked pleased,
though. We talked the most awful French together.

CHAPTER IV

TO-DAY HAS BEEN an absurd, grotesque, ridiculous day. Now it is eleven
o'clock at night. I am sitting in my little cupboard of a room, recalling it.
It began with my having to go to roulette to play for Polina Alexandrovna. I took the hundred and sixty friedrichs d'or, but on two
conditions: first, that I would not go halves — that is, if I won I would take

nothing for myself; and secondly, that in the evening Polina should explain to me why she needed to win, and how much money. I can't, in any case, suppose that it is simply for the sake of money. Evidently the money is needed, and as quickly as possible, for some particular object. She promised to explain, and I set off. In the gambling hall the crowd was awful. How insolent and how greedy they all were! I forced my way into the middle and stood near the croupier; then I began timidly experimenting, staking two or three coins at a time. Meanwhile, I kept quiet and looked on; it seemed to me that calculation meant very little, and had by no means the importance attributed to it by some players. They sit with papers before them scrawled over in pencil, note the strokes, reckon, deduce the chances, calculate, finally stake and — lose exactly as we simple mortals who play without calculations. On the other hand, I drew one conclusion which I believe to be correct: that is, though there is no system, there really is a sort of order in the sequence of casual chances — and that, of course, is very strange. For instance, it happens that after the twelve middle numbers come the twelve later numbers; twice, for instance, it turns up on the twelve last numbers and passes to the twelve first numbers. After falling on the twelve first numbers, it passes again to numbers in the middle third, turns up three or four times in succession on numbers between thirteen and twenty-four, and again passes to numbers in the last third; then, after turning up two numbers between twenty-five and thirty-six, it passes to a number among the first twelve, turns up once again on a number among the first third, and again passes for three strokes in succession to the middle numbers; and in that way goes on for an hour and a half or two hours. One, three and two — one, three and two. It's very amusing. One day or one morning, for instance, red will be followed by black and back again almost without any order, shifting every minute, so that it never turns up red or black for more than two or three strokes in succession. Another day, or another evening, there will be nothing but red over and over again, turning up, for instance, more than twenty-two times in succession, and so for a whole day. A great deal of this was explained to me by Mr. Astley, who spent the whole morning at the tables, but did not once put down a stake.

As for me, I lost every farthing very quickly. I staked straight off twenty friedrichs d'or on even and won, staked again and again won, and went on like that two or three times. I imagine I must have had about four hundred friedrichs d'or in my hands in about five minutes. At that point I ought to have gone away, but a strange sensation rose up in me, a sort of defiance of fate, a desire to challenge it, to put out my tongue at it. I laid down the largest stake allowed — four thousand guldens — and lost it.

Then, getting hot, I pulled out all I had left, staked it on the same number, and lost again, after which I walked away from the table as though I were stunned. I could not even grasp what had happened to me, and did not tell Polina Alexandrovna of my losing till just before dinner. I spent the rest of the day sauntering in the park.

At dinner I was again in an excited state, just as I had been three days before. The Frenchman and Mlle. Blanche were dining with us again. It appeared that Mlle. Blanche had been in the gambling hall that morning and had witnessed my exploits. This time she addressed me, it seemed, somewhat attentively. The Frenchman set to work more directly, and asked me: Was it my own money I had lost? I fancy he suspects Polina. In fact, there is something behind it. I lied at once and said it was.

The General was extremely surprised. Where had I got such a sum? I explained that I had begun with ten friedrichs d'or, that after six or seven times staking successfully on equal chances I had five or six hundred guldens, and that afterwards I had lost it all in two turns.

All that, of course, sounded probable. As I explained this I looked at Polina, but I could distinguish nothing from her face. She let me lie, however, and did not set it right; from this I concluded that I had to lie and conceal that I was in collaboration with her. In any case, I thought to myself, she is bound to give me an explanation, and promised me this morning to reveal something.

I expected the General would have made some remark to me, but he remained mute; I noticed, however, signs of disturbance and uneasiness in his face. Possibly in his straitened circumstances it was simply painful to him to hear that such a pile of gold had come into, and within a quarter of an hour had passed out of, the hands of such a reckless fool as me.

I suspect that he had a rather hot encounter with the Frenchman yesterday. They were shut up together talking for a long time. The Frenchman went away seeming irritated, and came to see the General again early this morning — probably to continue the conversation of the previous day.

Hearing what I had lost, the Frenchman observed bitingly, even spitefully, that one ought to have more sense. He added — I don't know why — that though a great many Russians gamble, Russians were not, in his opinion, well qualified even for gambling.

"In my mind," said I, "roulette is simply made for Russians."

And when at my challenge the Frenchman laughed contemptuously, I observed that I was, of course, right, for to speak of the Russians as gamblers was abusing them far more than praising them, and so I might be believed.

"On what do you base your opinion?" asked the Frenchman.

"On the fact that the faculty of amassing capital has, with the progress of history, taken a place — and almost the foremost place — among the virtues and merits of the civilized man of the West. The Russian is not only incapable of amassing capital, but dissipates it in a reckless and unseemly way. Nevertheless we Russians need money, too," I added, "and consequently we are very glad and very eager to make use of such means as roulette, for instance, in which one can grow rich all at once, in two hours, without work. That's very fascinating to us; and since we play badly, recklessly, without taking trouble, we usually lose!"

"That's partly true," observed the Frenchman complacently.

"No, it is not true, and you ought to be ashamed to speak like that of your country," observed the General, sternly and impressively.

"Allow me," I answered. "I really don't know which is more disgusting: Russian unseemliness or the German faculty of accumulation by honest toil."

"What an unseemly idea!" exclaimed the General.

"What a Russian idea!" exclaimed the Frenchman.

I laughed; I had an intense desire to provoke them.

"Well, I would prefer to dwell all my life in a Kirgiz tent," I cried, "than bow down to the German idol."

"What idol?" cried the General, beginning to be angry in earnest.

"The German faculty for accumulating wealth. I've not been here long, but yet all I have been able to observe and verify revolts my Tatar blood. My God! I don't want any such virtue! I succeeded yesterday in making a round of eight miles, and it's all exactly as in the edifying German picture-books: there is here in every house a *vater* horribly virtuous and extraordinarily honest — so honest that you are afraid to go near him. I can't endure honest people whom one is afraid to go near. Every such German *vater* has a family, and in the evening they read improving books aloud. Elms and chestnut trees rustle over the house. The sun is setting; there is a stork on the roof, and everything is extraordinarily practical and touching. . . . Don't be angry, General; let me tell it in a touching style. I remember how my father used to read similar books to my mother and me under the lime-trees in the garden. . . . So I am in a position to judge. And in what complete bondage and submission every such family is here. They all work like oxen and all save money like Jews. Suppose the *vater* has saved up so many guldens and is reckoning on giving his son a trade or a bit of land; to do so, he gives his daughter no dowry, and she becomes an old maid. To do so, the youngest son is sold into bondage or into the army, and the money is added to the family capital. This is actually done here; I've been making inquiries. All this is done from nothing but honesty, from such intense honesty that the younger son who is sold believes that he is sold from nothing but honesty: and that is the ideal when the victim himself rejoices at being led to the sacrifice. What more? Why, the elder son is no better off: he has an Amalia and their hearts are united, but they can't be married because the pile of guldens is not large enough. They, too, wait with perfect morality and good faith, and go to the sacrifice with a smile. Amalia's cheeks grow thin and hollow. At last, in twenty years, their prosperity is increased; the guldens have been honestly and virtuously accumulating. The *vater* gives his blessing to the forty-year-old son and his Amalia of thirty-five, whose chest has grown hollow and whose nose has turned red. . . . With that he weeps, reads them a moral sermon, and dies. The eldest son becomes himself a virtuous *vater* and begins the same story over again. In that way, in fifty or seventy years, the grandson of the first *vater* really has a considerable capital, and he leaves it to his son, and he to his, and he to his, till in five or six generations one of them is a Baron Rothschild or goodness knows who. Come, isn't that a majestic spectacle? A hundred or two hundred years of continuous toil, patience, intelligence, honesty, character, determination, prudence, the stork on the roof! What more do you want? Why, there's nothing loftier than that; and from that standpoint they are beginning to judge the whole world and to punish the guilty; that is, any who are ever so little unlike them. Well, so that's the point: I would rather waste my substance in the Russian style or grow rich at roulette. I don't care to be Goppe and Co in five generations. I want money for myself, and I don't look upon myself as something subordinate to capital and necessary to it. I know that I have been talking awful nonsense, but, never mind, such are my convictions."

"I don't know whether there is much truth in what you have been saying," said the General thoughtfully, "but I do know you begin to give yourself insufferable airs as soon as you are permitted to forget yourself in the least . . ."

As his habit was, he broke off without finishing. If our General began to speak of anything in the slightest degree more important than his ordinary everyday conversation, he never finished his sentences. The Frenchman listened carelessly with rather wide-open eyes; he had scarcely understood anything of what I had said. Polina gazed with haughty indifference. She seemed not to hear my words, or anything else that was said that day at table.

CHAPTER V

SHE WAS UNUSUALLY thoughtful, but directly we got up from table she bade me escort her for a walk. We took the children and went into the park towards the fountain.

As I felt particularly excited, I blurted out the crude and stupid question: why the Marquis de Grieux, our Frenchman, no longer escorted her when she went out anywhere, and did not even speak to her for days together.

"Because he is a rascal," she answered me strangely.

I had never heard her speak like that of De Grieux, and I received it in silence, afraid to interpret her irritability.

"Have you noticed that he is not on good terms with the General to-day?"

"You want to know what is the matter?" she answered drily and irritably. "You know that the General is completely mortgaged to him; all his property is his, and if Granny doesn't die, the Frenchman will come into possession of everything that is mortgaged to him."

"And is it true that everything is mortgaged? I had heard it, but I did not know that everything was."

"To be sure it is."

"Then farewell to Mlle. Blanche," said I. "She won't be the General's wife, then! Do you know, it strikes me the General is so much in love that he may shoot himself if Mlle. Blanche throws him over. It is dangerous to be so much in love at his age."

"I fancy that something will happen to him, too," Polina Alexandrovna observed musingly.

"And how splendid that would be!" I cried. "They couldn't have shown more coarsely that she was only marrying him for his money! There's no regard for decency, even; there's no ceremony about it whatever. That's wonderful! And about Granny — could there be anything more comic and sordid than to be continually sending telegram after telegram: 'Is she dead, is she dead?'? How do you like it, Polina Alexandrovna?"

"That's all nonsense," she said, interrupting me with an air of disgust. "I wonder at your being in such good spirits. What are you so pleased about? Surely not at having lost my money?"

"Why did you give it to me to lose? I told you I could not play for other people — especially for you! I obey you, whatever you order me to do, but I can't answer for the result. I warned you that nothing would come of it. Are you very much upset at losing so much money? What do you want so much for?"

"Why these questions?"

"Why, you promised to explain to me . . . Listen: I am absolutely convinced that when I begin playing for myself (and I've got twelve friedrichs d'or) I shall win. Then you can borrow as much from me as you like."

She made a contemptuous grimace.

"Don't be angry with me for such a suggestion," I went on. "I am so deeply conscious that I am nothing beside you — that is, in your eyes — that you may even borrow money from me. Presents from me cannot insult you. Besides, I lost yours."

She looked at me quickly, and seeing that I was speaking irritably and sarcastically, interrupted the conversation again.

"There's nothing of interest to you in my circumstances. If you want to know, I'm simply in debt. I've borrowed money and I wanted to repay it. I had the strange and mad idea that I should be sure to win here at the gambling table. Why I had the idea I can't understand, but I believed in it. Who knows, perhaps I believed it because no other alternative was left me."

"Or because it was quite *necessary* you should win. It's exactly like a drowning man clutching at a straw. You will admit that if he were not drowning he would not look at a straw as a branch of a tree."

Polina was surprised.

"Why," she said, "you were reckoning on the same thing yourself! A fortnight ago you said a great deal to me about your being absolutely convinced that you would win here at roulette, and tried to persuade me not to look upon you as mad; or were you joking then? But I remember you spoke so seriously that it was impossible to take it as a joke."

"That's true," I answered thoughtfully. "I am convinced to this moment that I shall win. I confess you have led me now to wonder why my senseless and unseemly failure to-day has not left the slightest doubt in me. I am still fully convinced that as soon as I begin playing for myself I shall be certain to win."

"Why are you so positive?"

"If you will have it — I don't know. I only know that I *must* win, that it is the only resource left me. Well, that's why, perhaps, I fancy I am bound to win."

"Then you, too, absolutely *must* have it, since you are so fanatically certain?"

"I bet you think I'm not capable of feeling that I *must* have anything?"

"That's nothing to me," Polina answered quietly and indifferently. "Yes, if you like. I doubt whether anything troubles you in earnest. You may be troubled, but not in earnest. You are an unstable person, not to be relied on. What do you want money for? I could see nothing serious in the reasons you brought forward the other day."

"By the way," I interrupted, "you said that you had to repay a debt. A fine debt it must be! To the Frenchman, I suppose?"

"What questions! You're particularly impertinent to-day. Are you drunk, perhaps?"

"You know that I consider myself at liberty to say anything to you, and sometimes ask you very candid questions. I repeat, I'm your slave, and one does not mind what one says to a slave, and cannot take offence at anything he says."

"And I can't endure that 'slave' theory of yours."

"Observe that I don't speak of my slavery because I want to be your slave. I simply speak of it as a fact which doesn't depend on me in the least."

"Tell me plainly, what do you want money for?"

"What do you want to know that for?"

"As you please," she replied, with a proud movement of her head. "You can't endure the 'slave' theory, but insist on slavishness: 'Answer and don't argue.' So be it. Why do I want money? you ask. How can you ask? Money is everything!"

"I understand that, but not falling into such madness from wanting it! You, too, are growing frenzied, fatalistic. There must be something behind it, some special object. Speak without beating about the bush; I wish it."

She seemed beginning to get angry, and I was awfully pleased at her questioning me with such heat.

"Of course there is an object," I answered, "but I don't know how to explain what it is. Nothing else but that with money I should become to you a different man, not a slave."

"What? How will you manage that?"

"How shall I manage it? What, you don't even understand how I could manage to make you look at me as anything but a slave? Well, that's just what I don't care for, such surprise and incredulity!"

"You said this slavery was a pleasure to you. I thought it was myself."

"You thought so!" I cried, with a strange enjoyment. "Oh, how delightful such *naïveté* is from you! Oh, yes, yes, slavery to you is a pleasure. There is — there is a pleasure in the utmost limit of humiliation and insignificance!" I went on maundering. "Goodness knows, perhaps there is in the knout when the knout lies on the back and tears the flesh. . . . But I should perhaps like to enjoy another kind of enjoyment. Yesterday, in your presence, the General thought fit to read me a lecture for the seven hundred roubles a year which perhaps I may not receive from him after all. The Marquis de Grieux raises his eyebrows and stares at me without noticing me. And I, perhaps, have a passionate desire to pull the Marquis de Grieux by the nose in your presence!"

"That's the speech of a milksop. One can behave with dignity in any position. If there is a struggle, it is elevating, not humiliating."

"That's straight out of a copybook! You simply take for granted that I don't know how to behave with dignity; that is, that perhaps I am a man of moral dignity, but that I don't know how to behave with dignity. You understand that that perhaps may be so. Yes, all Russians are like that; and do you know why? Because Russians are too richly endowed and many-sided to be able readily to evolve a code of manners. It is a question of good form. For the most part we Russians are so richly endowed that we need genius to evolve our code of manners. And genius is most often absent, for, indeed, it is a rarity at all times. It's only among the French, and perhaps some other Europeans, that the code of manners is so well defined that one may have an air of the utmost dignity and yet be a man of no moral dignity whatever. That's why good form means so much with them. A Frenchman will put up with an insult, a real, moral insult, without blinking, but he wouldn't endure a flip on the nose for anything, because that is a breach of the received code, sanctified for ages. That's why our Russian young ladies have such a weakness for Frenchmen, that their manners are so good. Though, to my thinking, they have no manners at all; it's simply the cock in them; *le coq gaulois*. I can't understand it, though; I'm not a woman. Perhaps cocks are nice. And, in fact, I've been talking nonsense, and you don't stop me. You must stop me more often. When I talk to you I long to tell you everything, everything, everything. I am oblivious of all good manners. I'll even admit that I have no manners, no moral qualities either. I tell you that. I don't even worry my head about moral qualities of any sort; everything has come to a standstill in me now; you know why. I have not one human idea in my head. For a long time past I've known nothing that has gone on in the world, either in Russia or here. Here I've been through Dresden, and I don't remember what Dresden was like. You know what has swallowed me up. As I have no hope whatever and am nothing in your eyes, I speak openly: I see nothing but you everywhere, and all the rest is naught to me. Why and how I love you I don't know. Perhaps you are not at all nice really, you know. Fancy! I don't know whether you are good or not, even to look at. You certainly have not a good heart; your mind may very well be ignoble."

"Perhaps that's how it is you reckon on buying me with money," she said, "because you don't believe in my sense of honour."

"When did I reckon on buying you with money?" I cried.

"You have been talking till you don't know what you are saying. If you don't think of buying me, you think of buying my respect with your money."

"Oh no, that's not it at all. I told you it was difficult for me to explain. You are overwhelming me. Don't be angry with my chatter. You know why you can't be angry with me: I'm simply mad. Though I really don't care, even if you are angry. When I am upstairs in my little garret I have only to remember and imagine the rustle of your dress, and I am ready to bite off my hands. And what are you angry with me for? For calling myself your slave? Make use of my being your slave, make use of it, make use of it! Do you know that I shall kill you one day? I shall kill you not because I shall cease to love you or be jealous, I shall simply kill you because I have an impulse to devour you. You laugh. . . ."

"I'm not laughing," she answered wrathfully. "I order you to be silent."

She stood still, almost breathless with anger. Upon my word, I don't know whether she was handsome, but I always liked to look at her when she stood facing me like that, and so I often liked to provoke her anger. Perhaps she had noticed this and was angry on purpose. I said as much to her.

"How disgusting!" she said, with an air of repulsion.

"I don't care," I went on. "Do you know, too, that it is dangerous for us to walk together? I often have an irresistible longing to beat you, to disfigure you, to strangle you. And what do you think — won't it come to that? You are driving me into brain fever. Do you suppose I am afraid of a scandal? Your anger — why, what is your anger to me? I love you without hope, and I know that after this I shall love you a thousand times more than ever. If ever I do kill you I shall have to kill myself, too. Oh, well, I shall put off killing myself as long as possible, so as to go on feeling this insufferable pain of being without you. Do you know something incredible? I love you *more* every day, and yet that is almost impossible. And how can I help being a fatalist? Do you remember the day before yesterday, on the Schlangenberg, I whispered at your provocation, 'Say the word, and I will leap into that abyss'? If you had said that word I should have jumped in then. Don't you believe that I would have leapt down?"

"What stupid talk!" she cried.

"I don't care whether it is stupid or clever!" I cried. "I know that in your presence I must talk, and talk, and talk — and I do talk. I lose all self-respect in your presence, and I don't care."

"What use would it be for me to order you to jump off the Schlangenberg?" she said in a dry and peculiarly insulting manner. "It would be absolutely useless to me."

"Splendid," I cried; "you said that splendid 'useless' on purpose to overwhelm me. I see through you. Useless, you say? But pleasure is always of use, and savage, unbounded power — if only over a fly — is a pleasure in its way, too. Man is a despot by nature, and loves to be a torturer. You like it awfully."

I remember she looked at me with peculiar fixed attention. My face must have expressed my incoherent and absurd sensations. I remember to this moment that our conversation actually was almost word for word exactly as I have described it here. My eyes were bloodshot. There were flecks of foam on my lips. And as for the Schlangenberg, I swear on my word of honour even now, if she had told me to fling myself down I should have flung myself down! If only for a joke she had said it, with contempt, if with a jeer at me she had said it, I should even then have leapt down!

"No, why? I believe you," she pronounced, as only she knows how to speak, with such contempt and venom, with such scorn that, by God, I could have killed her at the moment.

She risked it. I was not lying about that, too, in what I said to her.

"You are not a coward?" she asked me suddenly.

"Perhaps I am a coward. I don't know. . . . I have not thought about it for a long time."

"If I were to say to you, 'Kill this man,' would you kill him?"

"Whom?"

"Whom I choose."

"The Frenchman?"

"Don't ask questions, but answer. Whom I tell you. I want to know whether you spoke seriously just now?"

She waited for my answer so gravely and impatiently that it struck me as strange.

"Come, do tell me, what has been happening here?" I cried. "What are you afraid of — me, or what? I see all the muddle here for myself. You are the step-daughter of a mad and ruined man possessed by a passion for that devil — Blanche. Then there is this Frenchman, with his mysterious influence over you, and — here you ask me now so gravely . . . such a question. At any rate let me know, or I shall go mad on the spot and do something. Are you ashamed to deign to be open with me? Surely you can't care what I think of you?"

"I am not speaking to you of that at all. I asked you a question and I'm waiting for the answer."

"Of course I will kill any one you tell me to," I cried. "But can you possibly . . . could you tell me to do it?"

"Do you suppose I should spare you? I shall tell you to, and stand aside and look on. Can you endure that? Why, no, as though you could! You would kill him, perhaps, if you were told, and then you would come and kill me for having dared to send you."

I felt as though I were stunned at these words. Of course, even then I looked upon her question as half a joke, a challenge; yet she had spoken very earnestly. I was struck, nevertheless, at her speaking out so frankly, at her maintaining such rights over me, at her accepting such power over me and saying so bluntly: "Go to ruin, and I'll stand aside and look on." In those words there was something so open and cynical that to my mind it was going too far. That, then, was how she looked at me. This was something more than slavery or insignificance. If one looks at a man like that, one exalts him to one's own level, and absurd and incredible as all our conversation was, yet there was a throb at my heart.

Suddenly she laughed. We were sitting on a bench, before the playing children, facing the place where the carriages used to stop and people used to get out in the avenue before the Casino.

"Do you see that stout baroness?" she cried. "That is Baroness Burmerhelm. She has only been here three days. Do you see her husband—a tall, lean Prussian with a stick? Do you remember how he looked at us the day before yesterday? Go up to the Baroness at once, take off your hat, and say something to her in French."

"Why?"

"You swore that you would jump down the Schlangenberg; you swear you are ready to kill any one if I tell you. Instead of these murders and tragedies I only want to laugh. Go without discussing it. I want to see the Baron thrash you with his stick."

"You challenge me; you think I won't do it?"

"Yes, I do challenge you. Go; I want you to!"

"By all means, I am going, though it's a wild freak. Only, I say, I hope it won't be unpleasant for the General, and through him for you. Upon my honour, I am not thinking of myself, but of you and the General. And what a mad idea to insult a woman!"

"Yes, you are only a chatterer, as I see," she said contemptuously. "Your eyes were fierce and bloodshot, but perhaps that was only because you had too much wine at dinner. Do you suppose that I don't understand that it is stupid and vulgar, and that the General would be angry? I simply want to laugh; I want to, and that's all about it! And what should you insult a woman for? Why, just to be thrashed."

I turned and went in silence to carry out her commission. Of course it was stupid, and of course I did not know how to get out of it, but as I began to get closer to the Baroness I remember, as it were, something

within myself urging me on; it was an impulse of schoolboyish mischief.
Besides, I was horribly overwrought, and felt just as though I were drunk.

CHAPTER VI

NOW TWO DAYS have passed since that stupid day. And what a noise and
fuss and talk and uproar there was! And how unseemly and disgraceful,
how stupid and vulgar, it was! And I was the cause of it all. Yet at times
it's laughable — to me, at any rate. I can't make up my mind what
happened to me, whether I really was in a state of frenzy, or whether it
was a momentary aberration and I behaved disgracefully till I was pulled
up. At times it seemed to me that my mind was giving way. And at times
it seems to me that I have not outgrown childhood and schoolboyish-
ness, and that it was simply a crude schoolboy's prank.

It was Polina, it was all Polina! Perhaps I shouldn't have behaved like a
schoolboy if it hadn't been for her. Who knows? perhaps I did it out of
despair (stupid as it seems, though, to reason like that). And I don't
understand, I don't understand what there is fine in her! She is fine,
though; she is; I believe she's fine. She drives other men off their heads,
too. She's tall and graceful, only very slender. It seems to me you could
tie her in a knot or bend her double. Her foot is long and narrow —
tormenting. Tormenting is just what it is. Her hair has a reddish tint. Her
eyes are regular cat's eyes, but how proudly and disdainfully she can look
with them. Four months ago, when I had only just come, she was talking
hotly for a long while one evening with De Grieux in the drawing-room,
and looked at him in such a way . . . that afterwards, when I went up to
my room to go to bed, I imagined that she must have just given him a
slap in the face. She stood facing him and looked at him. It was from that
evening that I loved her.

To come to the point, however.

I stepped off the path into the avenue, and stood waiting for the Baron
and the Baroness. When they were five paces from me I took off my hat
and bowed.

I remember the Baroness was wearing a light grey dress of immense
circumference, with flounces, a crinoline, and a train. She was short
and exceptionally stout, with such a fearful double chin that she seemed
to have no neck. Her face was crimson. Her eyes were small, spiteful and
insolent. She walked as though she were doing an honour to all be-
holders. The Baron was lean and tall. Like most Germans, he had a wry
face covered with thousands of fine wrinkles, and wore spectacles; he
was about forty-five. His legs seemed to start from his chest: that's a sign

of race. He was as proud as a peacock. He was rather clumsy. There was something like a sheep in the expression of his face that would pass with them for profundity.

All this flashed upon my sight in three seconds.

My bow and the hat in my hand gradually arrested their attention. The Baron slightly knitted his brows. The Baroness simply sailed straight at me.

"*Madame la baronne*," I articulated distinctly, emphasizing each word, "*j'ai l'honneur d'être votre esclave*."

Then I bowed, replaced my hat, and walked past the Baron, turning my face towards him with a polite smile.

She had told me to take off my hat, but I had bowed and behaved like an impudent schoolboy on my own account. Goodness knows what impelled me to! I felt as though I were plunging into space.

"*Hein!*" cried, or rather croaked, the Baron, turning towards me with angry surprise.

I turned and remained in respectful expectation, still gazing at him with a smile. He was evidently perplexed, and raised his eyebrows as high as they would go. His face grew darker and darker. The Baroness, too, turned towards me, and she, too, stared in wrathful surprise. The passers-by began to look on. Some even stopped.

"*Hein!*" the Baron croaked again, with redoubled gutturalness and redoubled anger.

"*Ja wohl!*" I drawled, still looking him straight in the face.

"*Sind sie rasend?*" he cried, waving his stick and beginning, I think, to be a little nervous. He was perhaps perplexed by my appearance. I was very well, even foppishly, dressed, like a man belonging to the best society.

"*Ja wo-o-ohl!*" I shouted suddenly at the top of my voice, drawling the *o* like the Berliners, who use the expression *ja wohl* in every sentence, and drawl the letter *o* more or less according to the shade of their thought or feeling.

The Baron and Baroness turned away quickly and almost ran away from me in terror. Of the spectators, some were talking, others were gazing at me in amazement. I don't remember very clearly, though.

I turned and walked at my ordinary pace to Polina Alexandrovna.

But when I was within a hundred paces of her seat, I saw her get up and walk with the children towards the hotel.

I overtook her at the door.

"I have performed . . . the foolery," I said, when I reached her.

"Well, what of it? Now you can get out of the scrape," she answered. She walked upstairs without even glancing at me.

I spent the whole evening walking about the park. I crossed the park and then the wood beyond and walked into another state. In a cottage I had an omelette and some wine; for that idyllic repast they extorted a whole thaler and a half.

It was eleven o'clock before I returned home. I was at once summoned to the General.

Our party occupied two suites in the hotel; they have four rooms. The first is a big room — a drawing-room with a piano in it. The next, also a large room, is the General's study. Here he was awaiting me, standing in the middle of the room in a majestic pose. De Grieux sat lolling on the sofa.

"Allow me to ask you, sir, what have you been about?" began the General, addressing me.

"I should be glad if you would go straight to the point, General," said I. "You probably mean to refer to my encounter with a German this morning?"

"A German? That German was Baron Burmerhelm, a very important personage! You insulted him and the Baroness."

"Not in the least."

"You alarmed them, sir!" cried the General.

"Not a bit of it. When I was in Berlin the sound was for ever in my ears of that *ja wohl*, continually repeated at every word and disgustingly drawled out by them. When I met them in the avenue that *ja wohl* suddenly came into my mind, I don't know why, and — well, it had an irritating effect on me . . . Besides, the Baroness, who has met me three times, has the habit of walking straight at me as though I were a worm who might be trampled underfoot. You must admit that I, too, may have my proper pride. I took off my hat and said politely (I assure you I said it politely): '*Madame, j'ai l'honneur d'être votre esclave.*' When the Baron turned round and said, '*Hein!*' I felt an impulse to shout, '*Ja wohl!*' I shouted it twice: the first time in an ordinary tone, and the second — I drawled it as much as I could. That was all."

I must own I was intensely delighted at this extremely schoolboyish explanation. I had a strange desire to make the story as absurd as possible in the telling.

And as I went on, I got more and more to relish it.

"Are you laughing at me?" cried the General. He turned to the Frenchman and explained to him in French that I was positively going out of my way to provoke a scandal! De Grieux laughed contemptuously and shrugged his shoulders.

"Oh, don't imagine that; it was not so at all!" I cried. "My conduct was wrong, of course; I confess that with the utmost candour. My behaviour

may even be called a stupid and improper schoolboy prank, but —
nothing more. And do you know, General, I heartily regret it. But there
is one circumstance which, to my mind at least, almost saves me from
repentance. Lately, for the last fortnight, indeed, I've not been feeling
well: I have felt ill, nervous, irritable, moody, and on some occasions I
lose all control of myself. Really, I've sometimes had an intense impulse
to attack the Marquis de Grieux and . . . However, there's no need to say,
he might be offended. In short, it's the sign of illness. I don't know
whether the Baroness Burmerhelm will take this fact into consideration
when I beg her pardon (for I intend to apologize). I imagine she will not
consider it, especially as that line of excuse has been somewhat abused
in legal circles of late. Lawyers have taken to arguing in criminal cases
that their clients were not responsible at the moment of their crime, and
that it was a form of disease. 'He killed him,' they say, 'and has no
memory of it.' And only imagine, General, the medical authorities
support them — and actually maintain that there are illnesses, temporary aberrations in which a man scarcely remembers anything, or has
only a half or a quarter of his memory. But the Baron and Baroness are
people of the older generation; besides, they are Prussian *junkers* and
landowners, and so are probably unaware of this advance in the world of
medical jurisprudence, and will not accept my explanation. What do
you think, General?"

"Enough, sir," the General pronounced sharply, with surprised indignation; "enough! I will try once for all to rid myself of your mischievous
pranks. You are not going to apologize to the Baron and Baroness. Any
communication with you, even though it were to consist solely of your
request for forgiveness, would be beneath their dignity. The Baron has
learnt that you are a member of my household; he has already had an
explanation with me at the Casino, and I assure you that he was within
an ace of asking me to give him satisfaction. Do you understand what
you have exposed me to — me, sir? I — I was forced to ask the Baron's
pardon, and gave him my word that immediately, this very day, you
would cease to be a member of my household."

"Allow me, allow me, General; then did he insist on that himself, that
I should cease to belong to your household, as you were pleased to
express it?"

"No, but I considered myself bound to give him that satisfaction, and,
of course, the Baron was satisfied. We must part, sir. There is what is
owing to you, four friedrichs d'or and three florins, according to the
reckoning here. Here is the money, and here is the note of the account;
you can verify it. Good-bye. From this time forth we are strangers. I've
had nothing but trouble and unpleasantness from you. I will call the

kellner and inform him from this day forth that I am not responsible for your hotel expenses. I have the honour to remain your obedient servant."

I took the money and the paper upon which the account was written in pencil, bowed to the General, and said to him very seriously —

"General, the matter cannot end like this. I am very sorry that you were put into an unpleasant position with the Baron, but, excuse me, you were to blame for it yourself. Why did you take it upon yourself to be responsible for me to the Baron? What is the meaning of the expression that I am a member of your household? I am simply a teacher in your house, that is all. I am neither your son nor your ward, and you cannot be responsible for my actions. I am a legally responsible person, I am twenty-five, I am a graduate of the university, I am a nobleman, I am not connected with you in any way. Nothing but my unbounded respect for your dignity prevents me now from demanding from you the fullest explanation and satisfaction for taking upon yourself the right to answer for me."

The General was so much amazed that he flung up his hands, then turned suddenly to the Frenchman and hurriedly informed him that I had just all but challenged him to a duel.

The Frenchman laughed aloud.

"But I am not going to let the Baron off," I said, with complete composure, not in the least embarrassed by M. de Grieux's laughter; "and as, General, you consented to listen to the Baron's complaint to-day and have taken up his cause, and have made yourself, as it were, a party in the whole affair, I have the honour to inform you that no later than to-morrow morning I shall ask the Baron on my own account for a formal explanation of the reasons which led him to apply to other persons — as though I were unable or unfit to answer for myself."

What I foresaw happened. The General, hearing of this new absurdity, became horribly nervous.

"What, do you mean to keep up this damnable business?" he shouted. "What a position you are putting me in — good heavens! Don't dare, don't dare, sir, or, I swear! . . . There are police here, too, and I . . . I . . . in fact, by my rank . . . and the Baron's, too . . . in fact, you shall be arrested and turned out of the state by the police, to teach you not to make a disturbance. Do you understand that, sir?" And although he was breathless with anger, he was also horribly frightened.

"General," I answered, with a composure that was insufferable to him, "you can't arrest any one for making a disturbance before they have made a disturbance. I have not yet begun to make my explanations to the Baron, and you don't know in the least in what form or on what grounds I intend to proceed. I only wish to have an explanation of a position insulting to me, *i. e.* that I am under the control of a person who has authority over my freedom of action. There is no need for you to be so anxious and uneasy."

"For goodness' sake, for goodness' sake, Alexey Ivanovitch, drop this insane intention!" muttered the General, suddenly changing his wrathful tone for one of entreaty, and even clutching me by the hand. "Fancy what it will lead to! Fresh unpleasantness! You must see for yourself that I must be particular here . . . particularly now! particularly now! . . . Oh, you don't know, you don't know all my circumstances! . . . When we leave this place I shall be willing to take you back again; I was only speaking of now, in fact — of course, you understand there are reasons!" he cried in despair. "Alexey Ivanovitch, Alexey Ivanovitch . . ."

Retreating to the door, I begged him more earnestly not to worry himself, promised him that everything should go off well and with propriety, and hastily withdrew.

The Russian abroad is sometimes too easily cowed, and is horribly afraid of what people will say, how they will look at him, and whether this or that will be the proper thing. In short, they behave as though they were in corsets, especially those who have pretensions to consequence. The thing that pleases them most is a certain established traditional etiquette, which they follow slavishly in hotels, on their walks, in assemblies, on a journey . . . But the General had let slip that, apart from this, there was a particular circumstance, that he must be "particular." That was why he so weakly showed the white feather and changed his tone with me. I took this as evidence and made a note of it; and, of course, he might have brought my folly to the notice of the authorities, so that I really had to be careful.

I did not particularly want to anger the General, however; but I did want to anger Polina. Polina had treated me so badly, and had thrust me into such a stupid position, that I could not help wanting to force her to beg me to stop. My schoolboyish prank might compromise her, too. Moreover, another feeling and desire was taking shape in me: though I might be reduced to a nonentity in her presence, that did not prove that I could not hold my own before other people, or that the Baron could thrash me. I longed to have the laugh against them all, and to come off with flying colours. Let them see! She would be frightened by the scandal and call me back again, or, even if she didn't, at least she would see that I could hold my own.

(A wonderful piece of news! I have just heard from the nurse, whom I met on the stairs, that Marya Filippovna set off to-day, entirely alone, by the evening train to Karlsbad to see her cousin. What's the meaning of that? Nurse says that she has long been meaning to go; but how was it no one knew of it? Though perhaps I was the only one who did not know it: The nurse let slip that Marya Filippovna had words with the General the day before yesterday. I understand. No doubt that is Mlle. Blanche. Yes, something decisive is coming.)

CHAPTER VII

IN THE MORNING I called for the *kellner* and told him to make out a separate bill for me. My room was not such an expensive one as to make me feel alarmed and anxious to leave the hotel. I had sixteen friedrichs d'or, and there . . . there perhaps was wealth! Strange to say, I have not won yet, but I behave, I feel and think like a rich man, and cannot imagine anything else.

In spite of the early hour I intended to go at once to see Mr. Astley at the Hôtel d'Angleterre, which was quite close by, when suddenly De Grieux came in to me. That had never happened before, and, what is more, that gentleman and I had for some time past been on very queer and strained terms. He openly displayed his contempt for me, even tried not to conceal it; and I — I had my own reasons for disliking him. In short, I hated him. His visit greatly surprised me. I at once detected that something special was brewing.

He came in very politely and complimented me on my room. Seeing that I had my hat in my hand, he inquired whether I could be going out for a walk so early. When he heard that I was going to see Mr. Astley on business, he pondered, he reflected, and his face assumed an exceedingly careworn expression.

De Grieux was like all Frenchmen; that is, gay and polite when necessary and profitable to be so, and insufferably tedious when the necessity to be gay and polite was over. A Frenchman is not often naturally polite. He is always polite, as it were, to order, with a motive. If he sees the necessity for being fantastic, original, a little out of the ordinary, then his freakishness is most stupid and unnatural, and is made up of accepted and long-vulgarized traditions. The natural Frenchman is composed of the most plebeian, petty, ordinary practical sense — in fact, he is one of the most wearisome creatures in the world. In my opinion, only the innocent and inexperienced — especially Russian young ladies — are fascinated by Frenchmen. To every decent person the conventionalism of the established traditions of drawing-room politeness, ease and gaiety are at once evident and intolerable.

"I have come to see you on business," he began, with marked directness, though with courtesy, "and I will not disguise that I have come as

n ambassador, or rather as a mediator, from the General. As I know
Russian very imperfectly I understood very little of what passed yesterday, but the General explained it to me in detail, and I confess . . ."

"But, listen, M. de Grieux," I interrupted; "here you have undertaken
to be a mediator in this affair. I am, of course, an *outchitel*, and have
never laid claim to the honour of being a great friend of this.family, nor
of being on particularly intimate terms with it, and so I don't know all
he circumstances; but explain: are you now entirely a member of the
family? You take such an interest in everything and are certain at once to
be a mediator . . ."

This question did not please him. It was too transparent for him, and
he did not want to speak out.

"I am connected with the General partly by business, partly by *certain
special* circumstances," he said drily. "The General has sent me to ask
you to abandon the intentions you expressed yesterday. All you thought
of doing was no doubt very clever; but he begged me to represent to you
that you would be utterly unsuccessful; what's more, the Baron will not
receive you, and in any case is in a position to rid himself of any further
unpleasantness on your part. You must see that yourself. Tell me, what is
the object of going on with it? The General promises to take you back
into his home at the first convenient opportunity, and until that time will
continue your salary, *vos appointements*. That will be fairly profitable,
won't it?"

I retorted very calmly that he was rather mistaken; that perhaps I
shouldn't be kicked out at the Baron's, but, on the contrary, should be
listened to; and I asked him to admit that he had probably come to find
out what steps I was going to take in the matter.

"Oh heavens! Since the General is so interested, he will, of course, be
glad to know how you are going to behave, and what you are going to
do."

I proceeded to explain, and he began listening, stretching himself at
his ease and inclining his head on one side towards me, with an obvious,
undisguised expression of irony on his face. Altogether he behaved very
loftily. I tried with all my might to pretend that I took a very serious view
of the matter. I explained that since the Baron had addressed a complaint of me to the General as though I were the latter's servant, he had,
in the first place, deprived me thereby of my position; and secondly, had
treated me as a person who was incapable of answering for himself and
who was not worth speaking to. Of course, I said, I felt with justice that I
had been insulted; however, considering the difference of age, position
in society, and so on, and so on (I could scarcely restrain my laughter at
this point), I did not want to rush into fresh indiscretion by directly

insisting on satisfaction from the Baron, or even proposing a duel to him; nevertheless, I considered myself fully entitled to offer the Baron, and still more the Baroness, my apologies, especially since of late I had really felt ill, overwrought, and, so to say, fanciful, and so on, and so on. However, the Baron had, by his applying to the General, which was a slight to me, and by his insisting that the General should deprive me of my post, put me in such a position that now I could not offer him and the Baroness my apologies, because he and the Baroness and all the world would certainly suppose that I came to apologize because I was frightened and in order to be reinstated in my post. From all this it followed that I found myself now compelled to beg the Baron first of all to apologize to me in the most formal terms; for instance, to say that he had no desire to insult me. And when the Baron said this I should feel that my hands were set free, and with perfect candour and sincerity I should offer him my apologies. In brief, I concluded, I could only beg the Baron to untie my hands.

"Fie! how petty and how far-fetched! And why do you want to apologize? Come, admit, *monsieur . . . monsieur . . .* that you are doing all this on purpose to vex the General . . . and perhaps you have some special object . . . *mon cher monsieur . . . pardon, j'ai oublié votre nom, M. Alexis? . . . N'est-ce pas?*"

"But, excuse me, *mon cher marquis*, what is it to do with you?"

"*Mais le général . . .*"

"But what about the General? He said something last night, that he had to be particularly careful . . . and was so upset . . . but I did not understand it."

"There is, there certainly is a particular circumstance," De Grieux caught me up in an insistent voice, in which a note of vexation was more and more marked. "You know Mlle. de Cominges . . . ?"

"That is, Mlle. Blanche?"

"Why, yes, Mlle. Blanche de Cominges . . . *et madame sa mère*. You see for yourself, the General . . . in short, the General is in love; in fact . . . in fact, the marriage may be celebrated here. And fancy, scandal, gossip . . ."

"I see no scandal or gossip connected with the marriage in this."

"But *le baron est si irascible, un caractère Prussien, vous savez, enfin il fera une querelle d'Allemand.*"

"With me, then, and not with you, for I no longer belong to the household . . ." (I tried to be as irrational as possible on purpose). "But, excuse me, is it settled, then, that Mlle. Blanche is to marry the General? What are they waiting for? I mean, why conceal this from us, at any rate from the members of the household?"

"I cannot . . . however, it is not quite . . . besides . . . you know, they are expecting news from Russia; the General has to make arrangements . . ."

"A! a! La baboulinka!"

De Grieux looked at me with hatred.

"In short," he interrupted, "I fully rely on your innate courtesy, on your intelligence, on your tact . . . You will certainly do this for the family in which you have been received like one of themselves, in which you have been liked and respected . . ."

"Excuse me, I've been dismissed! You maintain now that that is only in appearance; but you must admit, if you were told: 'I won't send you packing, but, for the look of the thing, kindly take yourself off.' . . . You see, it comes almost to the same thing."

"Well, if that's how it is, if no request will have any influence on you," he began sternly and haughtily, "allow me to assure you that steps will be taken. There are authorities here; you'll be turned out to-day — que diable! Un blanc-bec comme vous wants to challenge a personage like the Baron! And do you think that you will not be interfered with? And, let me assure you, nobody is afraid of you here! I have approached you on my own account, because you have been worrying the General. And do you imagine that the Baron will not order his flunkeys to turn you out of the house?"

"But, you see, I'm not going myself," I answered, with the utmost composure. "You are mistaken, M. de Grieux; all this will be done much more decorously than you imagine. I am just setting off to Mr. Astley, and I am going to ask him to be my intermediary; in fact, to be my second. The man likes me, and certainly will not refuse. He will go to the Baron, and the Baron will receive him. Even if I am an outchitel and seem to be something subordinate and, well, defenceless, Mr. Astley is a nephew of a lord, of a real lord; every one knows that — Lord Pibroch — and that lord is here. Believe me, the Baron will be courteous to Mr. Astley and will listen to him. And if he won't listen, Mr. Astley will look upon it as a personal affront (you know how persistent Englishmen are), and will send a friend to call on the Baron; he has powerful friends. You may reckon, now, upon things not turning out quite as you expect."

The Frenchman was certainly scared; all this was really very much like the truth, and so it seemed that I really might be able to get up a scandal.

"Come, I beg you," he said in a voice of actual entreaty, "do drop the whole business! It seems to please you that it will cause a scandal! It is not satisfaction you want, but a scandal! As I have told you, it is very amusing and even witty — which is perhaps what you are aiming at. But, in short," he concluded, seeing that I had got up and was taking my hat, "I've come to give you these few lines from a certain person; read it; I was charged to wait for an answer."

Saying this, he took out of his pocket a little note, folded and sealed with a wafer, and handed it to me.

It was in Polina's handwriting.

"I fancy that you intend to go on with this affair, but there are special circumstances which I will explain to you perhaps later; please leave off and give way. It is all such silliness! I need you, and you promised yourself to obey me. Remember the Schlangenberg; I beg you to be obedient, and, if necessary, I command you. — Your P.

"P.S. — If you are angry with me for what happened yesterday, forgive me."

Everything seemed to be heaving before my eyes when I read these lines. My lips turned white and I began to tremble. The accursed Frenchman watched me with an exaggerated air of discretion, with his eyes turned away as though to avoid noticing my confusion. He had better have laughed at me outright.

"Very good," I answered; "tell Mademoiselle that she may set her mind at rest. Allow me to ask you," I added sharply, "why you have been so long giving me this letter. Instead of chattering about all sorts of nonsense, I think you ought to have begun with that . . . if you came expressly with that object."

"Oh, I wanted . . . all this is so strange that you must excuse my natural impatience. I was in haste to learn from you in person what you intended to do. Besides, I don't know what is in that note, and I thought there was no hurry for me to give it to you."

"I understand: the long and the short of it is you were told only to give me the letter in case of the utmost necessity, and if you could settle it by word of mouth you were not to give it me. Is that right? Tell me plainly, M. de Grieux."

"*Peut-être*," he said, assuming an air of peculiar reserve, and looking at me with a peculiar glance.

I took off my hat; he took off his hat and went out. It seemed to me that there was an ironical smile on his lips. And, indeed, what else could one expect?

"We'll be quits yet, Frenchy; we'll settle our accounts," I muttered as I went down the stairs. I could not think clearly; I felt as though I had had a blow on my head. The air revived me a little.

Two minutes later, as soon as ever I was able to reflect clearly, two thoughts stood out vividly before me: *the first* was that such trivial incidents, that a few mischievous and far-fetched threats from a mere boy, had caused such *universal* consternation! The *second* thought was: what sort of influence had this Frenchman over Polina? A mere word from him and she does anything he wants — writes a note and even *begs* me. Of course, their relations have always been a mystery to me from the very beginning, ever since I began to know them; but of late I have noticed in her a positive aversion and even contempt for him, while he did not even look at her, was absolutely rude to her. I had noticed it. Polina herself had spoken of him to me with aversion; she had dropped some extremely significant admissions . . . so he simply had her in his power. She was in some sort of bondage to him.

CHAPTER VIII

ON THE PROMENADE, as it is called here, that is, in the chestnut avenue, I met my Englishman.

"Oh, oh!" he began, as soon as he saw me. "I was coming to see you, and you are on your way to me. So you have parted from your people?"

"Tell me, first, how it is that you know all this?" I asked in amazement. "Is it possible that everybody knows of it?"

"Oh, no, every one doesn't; and, indeed, it's not worth their knowing. No one is talking about it."

"Then how do you know it?"

"I know, that is, I chanced to learn it. Now, where are you going when you leave here? I like you and that is why I was coming to see you."

"You are a splendid man, Mr. Astley," said I (I was very much interested, however, to know where he could have learnt it), "and since I have not yet had my coffee, and most likely you have not had a good cup, come to the café in the Casino. Let us sit down and have a smoke there, and I will tell you all about it, and . . . you tell me, too . . ."

The café was a hundred steps away. They brought us some coffee. We sat down and I lighted a cigarette. Mr. Astley did not light one and, gazing at me, prepared to listen.

"I am not going anywhere. I am staying here," I began.

"And I was sure you would," observed Mr. Astley approvingly.

On my way to Mr. Astley I had not meant to tell him anything of my love for Polina, and, in fact, I expressly intended to say nothing to him about it. All that time I had hardly said one word to him about it. He was, besides, very reserved. From the first I noticed that Polina had made a great impression upon him, but he never uttered her name. But, strange to say, now no sooner had he sat down and turned upon me his fixed, pewtery eyes, I felt, I don't know why, a desire to tell him everything, that is, all about my love in all its aspects. I was talking to him for half an hour and it was very pleasant to me; it was the first time I had talked of it! Noticing that at certain ardent sentences he was embarrassed, I purposely exaggerated my ardour. Only one thing I regret: I said, perhaps, more than I should about the Frenchman. . . .

Mr. Astley listened, sitting facing me without moving, looking straight into my eyes, not uttering a word, a sound; but when I spoke of the Frenchman, he suddenly pulled me up and asked me, severely, whether I had the right to refer to this circumstance which did not concern me? Mr. Astley always asked questions very strangely.

"You are right. I am afraid not," I answered.

"You can say nothing definite, nothing that is not supposition about that Marquis and Miss Polina?"

I was surprised again at such a point-blank question from a man so reserved as Mr. Astley.

"No, nothing definite," I answered; "of course not."

"If so, you have done wrong, not only in speaking of it to me, but even in thinking of it yourself."

"Very good, very good; I admit it, but that is not the point now," I interrupted, wondering at myself. At this point I told him the whole of yesterday's story in full detail: Polina's prank, my adventure with the Baron, my dismissal, the General's extraordinary dismay, and, finally, I described in detail De Grieux's visit that morning. Finally I showed him the note.

"What do you deduce from all this?" I asked. "I came on purpose to find out what you think. For my part, I could kill that Frenchman, and perhaps I shall."

"So could I," said Mr. Astley. "As regards Miss Polina, you know . . . we may enter into relations even with people who are detestable to us if we are compelled by necessity. There may be relations of which you know nothing, dependent upon outside circumstances. I think you may set your mind at rest — to some extent, of course. As for her action yesterday, it was strange, of course; not that she wanted to get rid of you and expose you to the Baron's walking-stick (I don't understand why he did not use it, since he had it in his hand), but because such a prank is improper . . . for such an . . . exquisite young lady. Of course, she couldn't have expected that you would carry out her jesting wish so literally . . ."

"Do you know what?" I cried suddenly, looking intently at Mr. Astley. "It strikes me that you have heard about this already — do you know from whom? From Miss Polina herself!"

Mr. Astley looked at me with surprise.

"Your eyes are sparkling and I can read your suspicion in them," he said, regaining his former composure; "but you have no right whatever to express your suspicions. I cannot recognize the right, and I absolutely refuse to answer your question."

"Enough! There's no need," I cried, strangely perturbed, and not knowing why it had come into my head. And when, where and how could Mr. Astley have been chosen by Polina to confide in? Though, of late, indeed, I had, to some extent, lost sight of Mr. Astley, and Polina was always an enigma to me, such an enigma that now, for instance, after launching into an account of my passion to Mr. Astley, I was suddenly struck while I was speaking by the fact that there was scarcely anything positive and definite I could say about our relations. Everything was, on the contrary, strange, unstable, and, in fact, quite unique.

"Oh, very well, very well. I am utterly perplexed and there is a great deal I can't understand at present," I answered, gasping as though I were breathless. "You are a good man, though. And now, another matter, and I ask not your advice, but your opinion."

After a brief pause I began.

"What do you think? why was the General so scared? Why did he make such a to-do over my stupid practical joke? Such a fuss that even De Grieux thought it necessary to interfere (and he interferes only in the most important matters); visited me (think of that!), begged and besought me — he, De Grieux — begged and besought me! Note, finally, he came at nine o'clock, and by that time Miss Polina's letter was in his hands. One wonders when it was written. Perhaps they waked Miss Polina up on purpose! Apart from what I see clearly from this, that Miss Polina is his slave (for she even begs my forgiveness!) — apart from that, how is she concerned in all this, she personally; why is she so much interested? Why are they frightened of some Baron? And what if the General is marrying Mlle. Blanche Cominges? They say that, owing to that circumstance, they must be *particular*, but you must admit that this is somewhat too particular! What do you think? I am sure from your eyes you know more about it than I do!"

Mr. Astley laughed and nodded.

"Certainly. I believe I know much more about it than you," he said. "Mlle. Blanche is the only person concerned, and I am sure that is the absolute truth."

"Well, what about Mlle. Blanche?" I cried impatiently. (I suddenly had a hope that something would be disclosed about Mlle. Polina.)

"I fancy that Mlle. Blanche has at the moment special reasons for avoiding a meeting with the Baron and Baroness, even more an unpleasant meeting, worse still, a scandalous one."

"Well, well . . ."

"Two years ago Mlle. Blanche was here at Roulettenburg in the season. I was here, too. Mlle. Blanche was not called Mlle. de Cominges then, and her mother, Madame la maman Cominges, was non-existent then. Anyway, she was never mentioned. De Grieux — De Grieux was not here either. I cherish the conviction that, far from being relations, they have only very recently become acquainted. He — De Grieux — has only become a marquis very recently, too — I am sure of that from one circumstance. One may assume, in fact, that his name has not been De Grieux very long either. I know a man here who has met him passing under another name."

"But he really has a very respectable circle of acquaintances."

"That may be. Even Mlle. Blanche may have. But two years ago, at the request of that very Baroness, Mlle. Blanche was invited by the police to leave the town, and she did leave it."

"How was that?"

"She made her appearance here first with an Italian, a prince of some sort, with an historical name — Barberini, or something like it — a man covered with rings and diamonds, not false ones either. They used to drive about in a magnificent carriage. Mlle. Blanche used to play *trente et quarante*, at first winning, but her luck changed later on, as far as I remember. I remember one evening she lost a considerable sum. But, worse still, *un beau matin* her prince vanished; the horses and the carriage vanished, too; everything vanished. The bills owing at the hotels were immense. Mlle. Selma (she suddenly ceased to be Barberini, and became Mlle. Selma) was in the utmost despair. She was shrieking and wailing all over the hotel, and rent her clothes in her fury. There was a Polish count staying here at the hotel (all Polish travellers are counts), and Mlle. Selma, rending her garments and scratching her face like a cat with her beautiful perfumed fingers, made some impression on him. They talked things over, and by dinner-time she was consoled. In the evening he made his appearance at the Casino with the lady on his arm. As usual, Mlle. Selma laughed very loudly, and her manner was somewhat more free and easy than before. She definitely showed that she belonged to the class of ladies who, when they go up to the roulette table, shoulder the other players aside to clear a space for themselves. That's particularly *chic* among such ladies. You must have noticed it?"

"Oh, yes."

"It's not worth noticing. To the annoyance of the decent public they are not moved on here — at least, not those of them who can change a thousand-rouble note every day, at the roulette table. As soon as they cease to produce a note to change they are asked to withdraw, however. Mlle. Selma still went on changing notes, but her play became more unlucky than ever. Note that such ladies are very often lucky in their play; they have a wonderful self-control. However, my story is finished. One day the Count vanished just as the Prince had done. However, Mlle. Selma made her appearance at the roulette table alone; this time no one came forward to offer her his arm. In two days she had lost everything. After laying down her last louis d'or and losing it, she looked round, and saw, close by her, Baron Burmerhelm, who was scrutinizing her intently and with profound indignation. But Mlle. Selma, not noticing his indignation, accosted the Baron with that smile we all know so well, and asked him to put down ten louis d'or on the red for her. In consequence of a complaint from the Baroness she received that evening an invitation not to show herself at the Casino again. If you are surprised at my knowing all these petty and extremely improper details, it is because I have heard them from Mr. Fider, one of my relations, who carried off Mlle. Selma in his carriage from Roulettenburg to Spa that very evening. Now, remember, Mlle. Blanche wishes to become the General's wife; probably in order in future not to receive such invitations as that one from the police at the Casino, the year before last. Now she does not play; but that is because, as it seems, she has capital of her own which she lends out at a percentage to gamblers here. That's a much safer speculation. I even suspect that the luckless General is in debt to her. Perhaps De Grieux is, too. Perhaps De Grieux is associated with her. You will admit that, till the wedding, at any rate, she can hardly be anxious to attract the attention of the Baron and Baroness in any way. In short, in her position, nothing could be more disadvantageous than a scandal. You are connected with their party and your conduct might cause a scandal, especially as she appears in public every day either arm-in-arm with the General or in company with Miss Polina. Now do you understand?"

"No, I don't!" I cried, thumping the table so violently that the garçon ran up in alarm.

"Tell me, Mr. Astley," I said furiously. "If you knew all this story and, therefore, know positively what Mlle. Blanche de Cominges is, why didn't you warn me at least, the General, or, most of all, most of all, Miss Polina, who has shown herself here at the Casino in public, arm-in-arm with Mlle. Blanche? Can such a thing be allowed?"

"I had no reason to warn you, for you could have done nothing," Mr. Astley answered calmly. "Besides, warn them of what? The General knows about Mlle. Blanche perhaps more than I do, yet he still goes about with her and Miss Polina. The General is an unlucky man. I saw Mlle. Blanche yesterday, galloping on a splendid horse with M. de Grieux and that little Russian Prince, and the General was galloping after them on a chestnut. He told me in the morning that his legs ached, but he sat his horse well. And it struck me at that moment that he was an utterly ruined man. Besides, all this is no business of mine, and I have only lately had the honour of making Miss Polina's acquaintance. However" (Mr. Astley caught himself up), "I've told you already that I do not recognize your right to ask certain questions, though I have a genuine liking for you . . ."

"Enough," I said, getting up. "It is clear as daylight to me now, that Miss Polina knows all about Mlle. Blanche, but that she cannot part from her Frenchman, and so she brings herself to going about with Mlle. Blanche. Believe me, no other influence would compel her to go about with Mlle. Blanche and to beg me in her letter not to interfere with the Baron! Damn it all, there's no understanding it!"

"You forget, in the first place, that this Mlle. de Cominges is the General's *fiancée*, and in the second place that Miss Polina is the General's step-daughter, that she has a little brother and sister, the General's own children, who are utterly neglected by that insane man and have, I believe, been robbed by him."

"Yes, yes, that is so! To leave the children would mean abandoning them altogether; to remain means protecting their interests and, perhaps, saving some fragments of their property. Yes, yes, all that is true. But still, still! . . . Ah, now I understand why they are all so concerned about Granny!"

"About whom?" asked Mr. Astley.

"That old witch in Moscow who won't die, and about whom they are expecting a telegram that she is dying."

"Yes, of course, all interest is concentrated on her. Everything depends on what she leaves them! If he comes in for a fortune the General will marry, Miss Polina will be set free, and De Grieux . . ."

"Well, and De Grieux?"

"And De Grieux will be paid; that is all he is waiting for here."

"Is that all, do you think that is all he's waiting for?"

"I know nothing more." Mr. Astley was obstinately silent.

"But I do, I do!" I repeated fiercely. "He's waiting for the inheritance too, because Polina will get a dowry, and as soon as she gets the money will throw herself on his neck. All women are like that! Even the proudest of them turn into the meanest slaves! Polina is only capable of loving passionately: nothing else. That's my opinion of her! Look at her, particularly when she is sitting alone, thinking; it's something predes-

tined, doomed, fated! She is capable of all the horrors of life, and passion
. . . she . . . she . . . but who is that calling me?" I exclaimed suddenly.
"Who is shouting? I heard some one shout in Russian: Alexey
Ivanovitch! A woman's voice. Listen, listen!"

At this moment we were approaching the hotel. We had left the café
long ago, almost without noticing it.

"I did hear a woman calling, but I don't know who was being called; it
is Russian. Now I see where the shouts come from," said Mr. Astley. "It is
that woman sitting in a big armchair who has just been carried up the
steps by so many flunkeys. They are carrying trunks after her, so the train
must have just come in."

"But why is she calling me? She is shouting again; look, she is waving
to us."

"I see she is waving," said Mr. Astley.

"Alexey Ivanovitch! Alexey Ivanovitch! Mercy on us, what a dolt he
is!" came desperate shouts from the hotel steps.

We almost ran to the entrance. I ran up the steps and . . . my hands
dropped at my sides with amazement and my feet seemed rooted to the
ground.

CHAPTER IX

AT THE TOP of the broad steps at the hotel entrance, surrounded by
footmen and maids and the many obsequious servants of the hotel, in
the presence of the *ober-kellner* himself, eager to receive the exalted
visitor, who had arrived with her own servants and with so many trunks
and boxes, and had been carried up the steps in an invalid chair, was
seated — *Granny!* Yes, it was she herself, the terrible old Moscow lady
and wealthy landowner, Antonida Vassilyevna Tarasyevitchev, the
Granny about whom telegrams had been sent and received, who had
been dying and was not dead, and who had suddenly dropped upon us
in person, like snow on our heads. Though she was seventy-five and had
for the last five years lost the use of her legs and had to be carried about
everywhere in a chair, yet she had arrived and was, as always, alert,
captious, self-satisfied, sitting upright in her chair, shouting in a loud,
peremptory voice and scolding every one. In fact, she was exactly the
same as she had been on the only two occasions that I had the honour of
seeing her during the time I had been tutor in the General's family.
Naturally I stood rooted to the spot with amazement. As she was being
carried up the steps, she had detected me a hundred paces away, with
her lynx-like eyes, had recognized me and called me by my name,

which she had made a note of, once for all, as she always did. And this
was the woman they had expected to be in her coffin, buried, and
leaving them her property. That was the thought that flashed into my
mind. "Why, she will outlive all of us and every one in the hotel! But, my
goodness! what will our friends do now, what will the General do? She
will turn the whole hotel upside down!"

"Well, my good man, why are you standing with your eyes starting out
of your head?" Granny went on shouting to me. "Can't you welcome
me? Can't you say 'How do you do'? Or have you grown proud and
won't? Or, perhaps, you don't recognize me? Potapitch, do you hear?"
She turned to her butler, an old man with grey hair and a pink bald
patch on his head, wearing a dress-coat and white tie. "Do you hear? he
doesn't recognize me. They had buried me! They sent telegram upon
telegram to ask whether I was dead or not! You see, I know all about it!
Here, you see, I am quite alive."

"Upon my word, Antonida Vassilyevna, why should I wish you harm?"
I answered gaily, recovering myself. "I was only surprised . . . And how
could I help being surprised at such an unexpected . . ."

"What is there to surprise you? I just got into the train and came. The
train was comfortable and not jolting. Have you been for a walk?"

"Yes, I've been a walk to the Casino."

"It's pleasant here," said Granny, looking about her. "It's warm and
the trees are magnificent. I like that! Are the family at home? The
General?"

"Oh, yes, at this time they are sure to be all at home."

"So they have fixed hours here, and everything in style? They set the
tone. I am told they keep their carriage, *les seigneurs russes!* They spend
all their money and then they go abroad. And is Praskovya with them?"

"Yes, Polina Alexandrovna, too."

"And the Frenchy? Oh, well, I shall see them all for myself. Alexey
Ivanovitch, show me the way straight to him. Are you comfortable
here?"

"Fairly so, Antonida Vassilyevna."

"Potapitch, tell that dolt, the *kellner*, to give me a nice convenient set
of rooms, not too high up, and take my things there at once. Why are
they all so eager to carry me? Why do they put themselves forward? Ech,
the slavish creatures! Who is this with you?" she asked, addressing me
again.

"This is Mr. Astley," I answered.

"What Mr. Astley?"

"A traveller, a good friend of mine; an acquaintance of the General's, too."

"An Englishman. To be sure he stares at me and keeps his mouth shut. I like Englishmen, though. Well, carry me upstairs, straight to their rooms. Where are they?"

They carried Granny up; I walked up the broad staircase in front. Our procession was very striking. Every one we met stopped and stared. Our hotel is considered the best, the most expensive, and the most aristocratic in the place. Magnificent ladies and dignified Englishmen were always to be met on the staircase and in the corridors. Many people were making inquiries below of the *ober-kellner*, who was greatly impressed. He answered, of course, that this was a distinguished foreign lady, *Une russe, une comtesse, grande dame*, and that she was taking the very apartments that had been occupied the week before by *la grande duchesse de N*. Granny's commanding and authoritative appearance as she was carried up in the chair was chiefly responsible for the sensation she caused. Whenever she met any one fresh she scrutinized him inquisitively and questioned me about him in a loud voice. Granny was powerfully built, and though she did not get up from her chair, it could be seen that she was very tall. Her back was as straight as a board and she did not lean back in her chair. Her big grey head with its large, bold features was held erect; she had a positively haughty and defiant expression; and it was evident that her air and gestures were perfectly natural. In spite of her seventy-five years there was still a certain vigour in her face: and even her teeth were almost perfect. She was wearing a black silk dress and a white cap.

"She interests me very much," Mr. Astley, who was going up beside me, whispered to me.

"She knows about the telegrams," I thought. "She knows about De Grieux, too, but I fancy she does not know much about Mlle. Blanche as yet." I communicated this thought to Mr. Astley.

Sinful man that I was, after the first surprise was over, I was immensely delighted at the thunderbolt that we were launching at the General. I was elated: and I walked in front feeling very gay.

Our apartments were on the third floor. Without announcing her arrival or even knocking at the door, I simply flung it wide open and Granny was carried in, in triumph. All of them were, as by design, assembled in the General's study. It was twelve o'clock and, I believe, some excursion was being planned for the whole party. Some were to drive, others were to ride on horseback, some acquaintances had been asked to join the party. Besides the General and Polina, with the children and their nurse, there were sitting in the study De Grieux, Mlle. Blanche, again wearing her riding-habit, her mother, the little Prince, and a learned German traveller whom I had not seen before.

Granny's chair was set down in the middle of the room, three paces from the General. My goodness! I shall never forget the sensation! As we went in the General was describing something, while De Grieux was correcting him. I must observe that Mlle. Blanche and De Grieux had for the last few days been particularly attentive to the little Prince, *à la barbe du pauvre général*, and the tone of the party was extremely gay and genially intimate, though, perhaps, it was artificial. Seeing Granny, the General was struck dumb. His mouth dropped open and he broke off in the middle of a word. He gazed at her open-eyed, as though spellbound by the eye of a basilisk. Granny looked at him in silence, too, immovably, but what a triumphant, challenging and ironical look it was! They gazed at each other for ten full seconds in the midst of profound silence on the part of all around them. For the first moment De Grieux was petrified, but immediately afterwards a look of extreme uneasiness flitted over his face. Mlle. Blanche raised her eyebrows, opened her mouth and gazed wildly at Granny. The Prince and the learned German stared at the whole scene in great astonishment. Polina's eyes expressed the utmost wonder and perplexity, and she suddenly turned white as a handkerchief; a minute later the blood rushed rapidly into her face, flushing her cheeks. Yes, this was a catastrophe for all of them! I kept turning my eyes from Granny to all surrounding her and back again. Mr. Astley stood on one side, calm and polite as usual.

"Well, here I am! Instead of a telegram!" Granny broke the silence by going off into a peal of laughter. "Well, you didn't expect me?"

"Antonida Vassilyevna . . . Auntie . . . But how on earth . . ." muttered the unhappy General.

If Granny had remained silent for a few seconds longer, he would, perhaps, have had a stroke.

"How on earth what? I got into the train and came. What's the railway for? You all thought that I had been laid out, and had left you a fortune? You see, I know how you sent telegrams from here. What a lot of money you must have wasted on them! They cost a good bit from here. I simply threw my legs over my shoulders and came off here. Is this the Frenchman? M. de Grieux, I fancy?"

"*Oui, Madame,*" De Grieux responded; "*et croyez, je suis si enchanté . . . votre santé . . . c'est un miracle . . . vous voir ici . . . une surprise charmante. . . .*"

"*Charmante,* I daresay; I know you, you mummer. I haven't this much faith in you," and she pointed her little finger at him. "Who is this?" she asked, indicating Mlle. Blanche. The striking-looking Frenchwoman, in a riding-habit with a whip in her hand, evidently impressed her. "Some one living here?"

"This is Mlle. Blanche de Cominges, and this is her mamma, Madame de Cominges; they are staying in this hotel," I explained.

"Is the daughter married?" Granny questioned me without ceremony.

"Mlle. de Cominges is an unmarried lady," I answered, purposely speaking in a low voice and as respectfully as possible.

"Lively?"

"I do not understand the question."

"You are not dull with her? Does she understand Russian? De Grieux picked it up in Moscow. He had a smattering of it."

I explained that Mlle. de Cominges had never been in Russia.

"*Bonjour,*" said Granny, turning abruptly to Mlle. Blanche.

"*Bonjour, madame.*" Mlle. Blanche made an elegant and ceremonious curtsey, hastening, under the cover of modesty and politeness, to express by her whole face and figure her extreme astonishment at such a strange question and manner of address.

"Oh, she casts down her eyes, she is giving herself airs and graces; you can see the sort she is at once; an actress of some kind. I'm stopping here below in the hotel," she said, turning suddenly to the General. "I shall be your neighbour. Are you glad or sorry?"

"Oh, Auntie! do believe in my sincere feelings . . . of pleasure," the General responded. He had by now recovered himself to some extent, and as, upon occasion, he could speak appropriately and with dignity, and even with some pretension to effectiveness, he began displaying his gifts now. "We have been so alarmed and upset by the news of your illness. . . . We received such despairing telegrams, and all at once . . ."

"Come, you are lying, you are lying," Granny interrupted at once.

"But how could you" — the General, too, made haste to interrupt, raising his voice and trying not to notice the word "lying" — "how could you bring yourself to undertake such a journey? You must admit that at your age and in your state of health . . . at any rate it is all so unexpected that our surprise is very natural. But I am so pleased . . . and we all" (he began smiling with an ingratiating and delighted air) "will try our utmost that you shall spend your season here as agreeably as possible . . ."

"Come, that's enough; that's idle chatter; you are talking nonsense, as usual. I can dispose of my time for myself. Though I've nothing against you, I don't bear a grudge. You ask how I could come? What is there surprising about it? It was the simplest thing. And why are you so surprised? How are you, Praskovya? What do you do here?"

"How do you do, Granny?" said Polina, going up to her. "Have you been long on the journey?"

"Well, she's asked a sensible question — the others could say nothing but oh and ah! Why, you see, I lay in bed and lay in bed and was doctored and doctored, so I sent the doctors away and called in the sexton from St. Nicolas. He had cured a peasant woman of the same disease by means of hayseed. And he did me good, too. On the third day I was in a perspiration all day and I got up. Then my Germans gathered round again, put on their spectacles and began to argue. 'If you were to go abroad now,' said they, 'and take a course of the waters, all your symptoms would disappear.' And why shouldn't I? I thought. The fools of Zazhigins began sighing and moaning: 'Where are you off to?' they said. Well, so here I am! It took me a day to get ready, and the following week, on a Friday, I took a maid, and Potapitch, and the footman, Fyodor, but I sent Fyodor back from Berlin, because I saw he was not wanted, and I could have come quite alone. I took a special compartment and there are porters at all the stations, and for twenty kopecks they will carry you wherever you like. I say, what rooms he has taken!" she said in conclusion, looking about her. "How do you get the money, my good man? Why, everything you've got is mortgaged. What a lot of money you must owe to this Frenchman alone! I know all about it; you see, I know all about it!"

"Oh, Auntie. . . ." said the General, all confusion. "I am surprised, Auntie . . . I imagine that I am free to act . . . Besides, my expenses are not beyond my means, and we are here . . ."

"They are not? You say so! Then you must have robbed your children of their last farthing — you, their trustee!"

"After that, after such words," began the General, indignant, "I really don't know . . ."

"To be sure you don't! I'll be bound you are always at roulette here? Have you whistled it all away?"

The General was so overwhelmed that he almost spluttered in the rush of his feelings.

"Roulette! I? In my position . . . I? Think what you are saying, Auntie; you must still be unwell . . ."

"Come, you are lying, you are lying. I'll be bound they can't tear you away; it's all lies! I'll have a look to-day what this roulette is like. You, Praskovya, tell me where to go and what to see, and Alexey Ivanovitch here will show me, and you, Potapitch, make a note of all the places to go to. What is there to see here?" she said, addressing Polina again.

"Close by are the ruins of the castle; then there is the Schlangenberg."

"What is it, the Schlangenberg? A wood or what?"

"No, not a wood, it's a mountain; there is a peak there . . ."

"What do you mean by a peak?"

"The very highest point on the mountain. It is an enclosed place — the view from it is unique."

"What about carrying my chair up the mountain? They wouldn't be able to drag it up, would they?"

"Oh, we can find porters," I answered.

At this moment, Fedosya, the nurse, came up to greet Granny and brought the General's children to her.

"Come, there's no need for kissing! I cannot bear kissing children, they always have dirty noses. Well, how do you get on here, Fedosya?"

"It's very, very nice here, Antonida Vassilyevna," answered Fedosya. "How have you been, ma'am? We've been so worried about you."

"I know, you are a good soul. Do you always have visitors?" — she turned to Polina again. "Who is that wretched little rascal in spectacles?"

"Prince Nilsky," Polina whispered.

"Ah, a Russian. And I thought he wouldn't understand! Perhaps he didn't hear. I have seen Mr. Astley already. Here he is again," said Granny, catching sight of him. "How do you do?" — she turned to him suddenly.

Mr. Astley bowed to her in silence.

"Have you no good news to tell me? Say something! Translate that to him, Polina."

Polina translated it.

"Yes. That with great pleasure and delight I am looking at you, and very glad that you are in good health," Mr. Astley answered seriously, but with perfect readiness. It was translated to Granny and it was evident she was pleased.

"How well Englishmen always answer," she observed. "That's why I always like Englishmen. There's no comparison between them and Frenchmen! Come and see me," she said, addressing Mr. Astley again. "I'll try not to worry you too much. Translate that to him, and tell him that I am here below — here below — do you hear? Below, below," she repeated to Mr. Astley, pointing downwards.

Mr. Astley was extremely pleased at the invitation.

Granny looked Polina up and down attentively and with a satisfied air.

"I was fond of you, Praskovya," she said suddenly. "You're a fine wench, the best of the lot, and as for will — my goodness! Well, I have will too; turn round. That's not a false chignon, is it?"

"No, Granny, it's my own."

"To be sure. I don't care for the silly fashion of the day. You look very nice. I should fall in love with you if I were a young gentleman. Why don't you get married? But it is time for me to go. And I want to go out, for I've had nothing but the train and the train . . . Well, are you still cross?" she added, turning to the General.

"Upon my word, Auntie, what nonsense!" cried the General, delighted. "I understand at your age . . ."

"*Cette vieille est tombée en enfance*," De Grieux whispered to me.

"I want to see everything here. Will you let me have Alexey Ivanovitch?" Granny went on to the General.

"Oh, as much as you like, but I will myself . . . and Polina, M. de Grieux . . . we shall all think it a pleasure to accompany you."

"*Mais, madame, cela sera un plaisir*" . . . De Grieux addressed her with a bewitching smile.

"A *plaisir*, to be sure; you are absurd, my good sir. I am not going to give you any money, though," she added suddenly. "But now to my rooms; I must have a look at them, and then we'll go the round of everything. Come, lift me up." Granny was lifted up again and we all flocked downstairs behind her chair. The General walked as though stunned by a blow on the head. De Grieux was considering something. Mlle. Blanche seemed about to remain, but for some reason she made up her mind to come with the rest. The Prince followed her at once, and no one was left in the General's study but Madame de Cominges and the German.

CHAPTER X

AT WATERING-PLACES and, I believe, in Europe generally, hotel-keepers and *ober-kellners*, in assigning rooms to their visitors, are guided not so much by the demands and desires of the latter as by their own personal opinion of them, and, one must add, they are rarely mistaken. But for some reason I cannot explain, they had assigned Granny such a splendid suite that they had quite overshot the mark. It consisted of four splendidly furnished rooms with a bathroom, quarters for the servants and a special room for the maid, and so on. Some *grande duchesse* really had been staying in those rooms the week before, a fact of which the new occupant was informed at once, in order to enhance the value of the apartments. Granny was carried, or rather wheeled, through all the rooms, and she looked at them attentively and severely. The *ober-kellner*, an elderly man with a bald head, followed her respectfully at this first survey.

I don't know what they all took Granny to be, but apparently for a very important and, above all, wealthy lady. They put down in the book at once: "*Madame la générale princesse de Tarasyevitchev*," though Granny had never been a princess. Her servants, her special compartment in the train, the mass of useless bags, portmanteaus, and even chests that had come with Granny, probably laid the foundation of her prestige; while her invalid-chair, her abrupt tone and voice, her eccentric questions, which were made with the most unconstrained air that would tolerate no contradiction—in short, Granny's whole figure, erect, brisk, imperious—increased the awe in which she was held by all. As she looked at the rooms, Granny sometimes told them to stop her chair, pointed to some object in the furniture and addressed unexpected questions to the *ober-kellner*, who still smiled respectfully, though he was beginning to feel nervous. Granny put her questions in French, which she spoke, however, rather badly, so that I usually translated. The *ober-kellner's* answers for the most part did not please her and seemed unsatisfactory. And, indeed, she kept asking about all sorts of things quite irrelevant. Suddenly, for instance, stopping before a picture, a rather feeble copy of some well-known picture of a mythological subject, she would ask—

"Whose portrait is that?"

The *ober-kellner* replied that no doubt it was some countess.

"How is it you don't know? You live here and don't know. Why is it here? Why is she squinting?"

The *ober-kellner* could not answer these questions satisfactorily, and positively lost his head.

"Oh, what a blockhead!" commented Granny, in Russian.

She was wheeled on. The same performance was repeated with a Dresden statuette, which Granny looked at for a long time, and then ordered them to remove, no one knew why. Finally, she worried the *ober-kellner* about what the carpets in the bedroom cost, and where they had been woven! The *ober-kellner* promised to make inquiries.

"What asses," Granny grumbled, and concentrated her whole attention on the bed. "What a gorgeous canopy! Open the bed."

They opened the bed.

"More, more, turn it all over. Take off the pillows, the pillows, lift up the feather bed."

Everything was turned over. Granny examined it attentively.

"It's a good thing there are no bugs. Take away all the linen! Make it up with my linen and my pillows. But all this is too gorgeous. Such rooms are not for an old woman like me. I shall be dreary all alone. Alexey Ivanovitch, you must come and see me very often when your lessons with the children are over."

"I left the General's service yesterday," I answered, "and am living in the hotel quite independently."

"How is that?"

"A German of high rank, a Baron, with his Baroness, came here from Berlin the other day. I addressed him yesterday in German without keeping to the Berlin accent."

"Well, what then?"

"He thought it an impertinence and complained to the General, and yesterday the General discharged me."

"Why, did you swear at the Baron, or what? (though if you had it wouldn't have mattered!)"

"Oh, no. On the contrary, the Baron raised his stick to thrash me."

"And did you, sniveller, allow your tutor to be treated like that?" she said suddenly, addressing the General; "and turned him out of his place too! Noodles! you're all a set of noodles, as I see."

"Don't disturb yourself, Auntie," said the General, with a shade of condescending familiarity; "I can manage my own business. Besides, Alexey Ivanovitch has not given you quite a correct account of it."

"And you just put up with it?"—she turned to me.

"I meant to challenge the Baron to a duel," I answered, as calmly and as modestly as I could, "but the General opposed it."

"Why did you oppose it?"—Granny turned to the General again. ("And you can go, my good man; you can come when you are called," she said, addressing the *ober-kellner*; "no need to stand about gaping. I can't endure this Nürnberg rabble!")

The man bowed and went out, not, of course, understanding Granny's compliments.

"Upon my word, Auntie, surely a duel was out of the question."

"Why out of the question? Men are all cocks; so they should fight. You are all noodles, I see, you don't know how to stand up for your country. Come, take me up, Potapitch; see that there are always two porters: engage them. I don't want more than two. I shall only want them to carry me up and down stairs, and to wheel me on the levels in the street. Explain that to them; and pay them beforehand—they will be more respectful. You will always be with me yourself, and you, Alexey Ivanovitch, point out that Baron to me when we are out: that I may have a look at the von Baron. Well, where is the roulette?"

I explained that the roulette tables were in rooms in the Casino. Then followed questions: Were there many of them? Did many people play? Did they play all day long? How was it arranged? I answered at last, that she had much better see all this with her own eyes, and that it was rather difficult to describe it.

"Well, then, take me straight there! You go first, Alexey Ivanovitch!"

"Why, Auntie, don't you really mean to rest after your journey?" the General asked anxiously. He seemed rather flurried and, indeed, they all seemed embarrassed and were exchanging glances. Probably they all felt it rather risky and, indeed, humiliating to accompany Granny to the Casino, where, of course, she might do something eccentric, and in public; at the same time they all proposed to accompany her.

"Why should I rest? I am not tired and, besides, I've been sitting still for three days. And then we will go and see the springs and medicinal waters; where are they? And then . . . we'll go and see, what was it you said, Praskovya? — peak, wasn't it?"

"Yes, Granny."

"Well, peak, then, if it is a peak. And what else is there here?"

"There are a great many objects of interest, Granny," Polina exerted herself to say.

"Why don't you know them! Marfa, you shall come with me, too," she said, addressing her maid.

"But why should she come?" the General said fussily; "and in fact it's out of the question, and I doubt whether Potapitch will be admitted into the Casino."

"What nonsense! Am I to abandon her because she is a servant? She's a human being, too; here we have been on our travels for a week; she wants to have a look at things, too. With whom could she go except me? She wouldn't dare show her nose in the street by herself."

"But, Granny . . ."

"Why, are you ashamed to be with me? Then stay at home; you are not asked. Why, what a General! I am a General's widow myself. And why should you all come trailing after me? I can look at it all with Alexey Ivanovitch."

But De Grieux insisted that we should all accompany her, and launched out into the most polite phrases about the pleasure of accompanying her, and so on. We all started.

"*Elle est tombée en enfance,*" De Grieux repeated to the General; "*seule, elle fera des bêtises . . .*" I heard nothing more, but he evidently had some design, and, possibly, his hopes had revived.

It was half a mile to the Casino. The way was through an avenue of chestnuts to a square, going round which, they came out straight on the Casino. The General was to some extent reassured, for our procession, though somewhat eccentric, was, nevertheless, decorous and presentable. And there was nothing surprising in the fact of an invalid who could not walk putting in an appearance at the Casino; but, anyway, the General was afraid of the Casino; why should an invalid unable to walk, and an old lady, too, go into the gambling saloon? Polina and Mlle. Blanche walked on each side of the bath-chair. Mlle. Blanche laughed, was modestly animated and even sometimes jested very politely with Granny, so much so that the latter spoke of her approvingly at last. Polina, on the other side, was obliged to be continually answering Granny's innumerable questions, such as: "Who was that passed? Who was that woman driving past? Is it a big town? Is it a big garden? What are those trees? What's that hill? Do eagles fly here? What is that absurd-looking roof?" Mr. Astley walked beside me and whispered that he expected a great deal from that morning. Potapitch and Marfa walked in the background close behind the bath-chair, Potapitch in his swallow-tailed coat and white tie, but with a cap on his head, and Marfa (a red-faced maidservant, forty years old and beginning to turn grey) in a cap, cotton gown, and creaking goatskin slippers. Granny turned to them very often and addressed remarks to them. De Grieux was talking with an air of determination. Probably he was reassuring the General, evidently he was giving him some advice. But Granny had already pronounced the fatal phrase: "I am not going to give you money." Perhaps to De Grieux this announcement sounded incredible, but the General knew his aunt. I noticed that De Grieux and Mlle. Blanche were continually exchanging glances. I could distinguish the Prince and the German traveller at the further end of the avenue; they had stopped, and were walking away from us.

Our visit to the Casino was a triumph. The porters and attendants displayed the same deference as in the hotel. They looked at us, however, with curiosity. Granny began by giving orders that she should be wheeled through all the rooms. Some she admired, others made no impression on her; she asked questions about them all. At last we came to the roulette room. The lackeys, who stood like sentinels at closed doors, flung the doors wide open as though they were impressed.

Granny's appearance at the roulette table made a profound impression on the public. At the roulette tables and at the other end of the room, where there was a table with *trente et quarante*, there was a crowd of a hundred and fifty or two hundred players, several rows deep. Those who had succeeded in squeezing their way right up to the table, held fast, as they always do, and would not give up their places to any one until they had lost; for simple spectators were not allowed to stand at the tables and occupy the space. Though there were chairs set round the table, few of the players sat down, especially when there was a great crowd, because standing one could get closer and consequently pick out one's place and put down one's stake more conveniently. The second and the third rows pressed up upon the first, waiting and watching for their turn; but sometimes a hand would be impatiently thrust forward through the first row to put down a stake. Even from the third row people managed to seize chances of poking forward their stakes; consequently every ten or even five minutes there was some "scene" over disputed stakes at one end of the hall or another. The police of the Casino were, however, fairly good. It was, of course, impossible to prevent crowding; on the contrary, the owners were glad of the rush of people because it was profitable, but eight croupiers sitting round the table kept a vigilant watch on the stakes: they even kept count of them, and when disputes arose they could settle them. In extreme cases they called in the police, and the trouble was over in an instant. There were police officers in plain clothes stationed here and there among the players, so that they could not be recognized. They were especially on the look-out for thieves and professional pickpockets, who are very numerous at the roulette tables, as it affords them excellent opportunity for exercising their skill. The fact is, elsewhere thieves must pick pockets or break locks, and such enterprises, when unsuccessful, have a very troublesome ending. But in this case the thief has only to go up to the roulette table, begin playing, and all at once, openly and publicly, take another person's winnings and put them in his pocket. If a dispute arises, the cheat insists loudly that the stake was his. If the trick is played cleverly and the witnesses hesitate, the thief may often succeed in carrying off the money, if the sum is not a very large one, of course. In that case the croupiers or some one of the other players are almost certain to have been keeping an eye on it. But if the sum is not a large one, the real owner sometimes actually declines to keep up the dispute, and goes away shrinking from the scandal. But if they succeed in detecting a thief, they turn him out at once with contumely.

All this Granny watched from a distance with wild curiosity. She was much delighted at a thief's being turned out. *Trente et quarante* did not interest her very much; she was more pleased at roulette and the rolling of the little ball. She evinced a desire a last to get a closer view of the game. I don't know how it happened, but the attendants and other officious persons (principally Poles who had lost, and who pressed their services on lucky players and foreigners of all sorts) at once, and in spite of the crowd, cleared a place for Granny in the very middle of the table beside the chief croupier, and wheeled her chair to it. A number of visitors who were not playing, but watching the play (chiefly Englishmen with their families), at once crowded round the table to watch Granny from behind the players. Numbers of lorgnettes were turned in her direction. The croupiers' expectations rose. Such an eccentric person certainly seemed to promise something out of the ordinary. An old woman of seventy, who could not walk, yet wished to play, was, of course, not a sight to be seen every day. I squeezed my way up to the table too, and took my stand beside Granny. Potapitch and Marfa were left somewhere in the distance among the crowd. The General, Polina, De Grieux, and Mlle. Blanche stood aside, too, among the spectators.

At first Granny began looking about at the players. She began in a half whisper asking me abrupt, jerky questions. Who was that man and who was this woman? She was particularly delighted by a young man at the end of the table, who was playing for very high stakes, putting down thousands and had, as people whispered around, already won as much as forty thousand francs, which lay before him in heaps of gold and banknotes. He was pale; his eyes glittered and his hands were shaking; he was staking now without counting, by handfuls, and yet he kept on winning and winning, kept raking in and raking in the money. The attendants hung about him solicitously, set a chair for him, cleared a place round him that he might have more room, that he might not be crowded — all this in expectation of a liberal tip. Some players, after they have won, tip the attendants without counting a handful of coins in their joy. A Pole had already established himself at his side, and was deferentially but continually whispering to him, probably telling him what to stake on, advising and directing his play — of course, he, too, expecting a tip later on! But the player scarcely looked at him. He staked at random and kept winning. He evidently did not know what he was doing.

Granny watched him for some minutes.

"Tell him," Granny said suddenly, growing excited and giving me a poke, "tell him to give it up, to take his money quickly and go away. He'll lose it all directly, he'll lose it all!" she urged, almost breathless with agitation. "Where's Potapitch? Send Potapitch to him. Come, tell him, tell him," she went on, poking me. "Where is Potapitch? *Sortez! Sortez!*" — she began herself shouting to the young man.

I bent down to her and whispered resolutely that she must not shout like this here, that even talking aloud was forbidden, because it hindered counting and that we should be turned out directly.

"How vexatious! The man's lost! I suppose it's his own doing. . . . I can't look at him, it quite upsets me. What a dolt!" and Granny made haste to turn in another direction.

On the left, on the other side of the table, there was conspicuous among the players a young lady, and beside her a sort of dwarf. Who this dwarf was, and whether he was a relation or brought by her for the sake of effect, I don't know. I had noticed the lady before; she made her appearance at the gambling table every day, at one o'clock in the afternoon, and went away exactly at two; she always played for an hour. She was already known, and a chair was set for her at once. She took out of her pocket some gold, some thousand-franc notes, and began staking quietly, coolly, prudently, making pencil notes on a bit of paper of the numbers about which the chances grouped themselves, and trying to work out a system. She staked considerable sums. She used to win every day — one, two, or at the most three thousand francs — not more, and instantly went away. Granny scrutinized her for a long time.

"Well, that one won't lose! That one there won't lose! Of what class is she! Do you know? Who is she?"

"She must be a Frenchwoman, of a certain class, you know," I whispered.

"Ah, one can tell the bird by its flight. One can see she has a sharp claw. Explain to me now what every turn means and how one has to bet!"

I explained as far as I could to Granny all the various points on which one could stake: *rouge et noir, pair et impair, manque et passe*, and finally the various subtleties in the system of the numbers. Granny listened attentively, remembered, asked questions, and began to master it. One could point to examples of every kind, so that she very quickly and readily picked up a great deal.

"But what is zéro? You see that croupier, the curly-headed one, the chief one, showed zéro just now? And why did he scoop up everything that was on the table? Such a heap, he took it all for himself. What is the meaning of it?"

"Zéro, Granny, means that the bank wins all. If the little ball falls on zéro, everything on the table goes to the bank. It is true you can stake your money so as to keep it, but the bank pays nothing."

"You don't say so! And shall I get nothing?"

"No, Granny, if before this you had staked on zéro you would have got thirty-five times what you staked."

"What! thirty-five times, and does it often turn up? Why don't they stake on it, the fools."

"There are thirty-six chances against it, Granny."

"What nonsense. Potapitch! Potapitch! Stay, I've money with me— here." She took out of her pocket a tightly packed purse, and picked out of it a friedrich d'or. "Stake it on the zéro at once."

"Granny, zéro has only just turned up," I said; "so now it won't turn up for a long time. You will lose a great deal; wait a little, anyway."

"Oh, nonsense; put it down!"

"As you please, but it may not turn up again till the evening. You may go on staking thousands; it has happened."

"Oh, nonsense, nonsense. If you are afraid of the wolf you shouldn't go into the forest. What? Have I lost? Stake again!"

A second friedrich d'or was lost: she staked a third. Granny could scarcely sit still in her seat. She stared with feverish eyes at the little ball dancing on the spokes of the turning wheel. She lost a third, too. Granny was beside herself, she could not sit still, she even thumped on the table with her fist when the croupier announced, "trente-six" instead of the zéro she was expecting.

"There, look at it," said Granny angrily; "isn't that cursed little zéro coming soon? As sure as I'm alive, I'll sit here till zéro does come! It's that cursed curly-headed croupier's doing; he'll never let it come! Alexey

Ivanovitch, stake two gold pieces at once! Staking as much as you do, even if zéro does come you'll get nothing by it."

"Granny!"

"Stake, stake! it is not your money."

I staked two friedrichs d'or. The ball flew about the wheel for a long time, at last it began dancing about the spokes. Granny was numb with excitement, and squeezed my fingers, and all at once—

"Zéro!" boomed the croupier.

"You see, you see!"—Granny turned to me quickly, beaming and delighted. "I told you so. The Lord Himself put it into my head to stake those two gold pieces! Well, how much do I get now? Why don't they give it me. Potapitch, Marfa, where are they? Where have all our people got to? Potapitch, Potapitch!"

"Granny, afterwards," I whispered; "Potapitch is at the door, they won't let him in. Look, Granny, they are giving you the money, take it!" A heavy roll of printed blue notes, worth fifty friedrichs d'or, was thrust towards Granny and twenty friedrichs d'or were counted out to her. I scooped it all up in a shovel and handed it to Granny.

"*Faites le jeu, messieurs! Faites le jeu, messieurs! Rien ne va plus?*" called the croupier, inviting the public to stake, and preparing to turn the wheel.

"Heavens! we are too late. They're just going to turn it. Put it down, put it down!" Granny urged me in a flurry. "Don't dawdle, make haste!" She was beside herself and poked me with all her might.

"What am I to stake it on, Granny?"

"On zéro, on zéro! On zéro again! Stake as much as possible! How much have we got altogether. Seventy friedrichs d'or. There's no need to spare it. Stake twenty friedrichs d'or at once."

"Think what you are doing, Granny! sometimes it does not turn up for two hundred times running! I assure you, you may go on staking your whole fortune."

"Oh, nonsense, nonsense! Put it down! How your tongue does wag! I know what I'm about." Granny was positively quivering with excitement.

"By the regulations it's not allowed to stake more than twelve roubles on zéro at once, Granny; here I have staked that."

"Why is it not allowed? Aren't you lying? Monsieur! Monsieur!"—she nudged the croupier, who was sitting near her on the left, and was about to set the wheel turning. "*Combien zéro? Douze? Douze?*"

I immediately interpreted the question in French.

"*Oui, madame,*" the croupier confirmed politely; "as the winnings from no single stake must exceed four thousand florins by the regulations," he added in explanation.

"Well, there's no help for it, stake twelve."

"*Le jeu est fait*," cried the croupier. The wheel rotated, and thirty turned up. She had lost.

"Again, again, again! Stake again!" cried Granny. I no longer resisted, and, shrugging my shoulders, staked another twelve friedrichs d'or. The wheel turned a long time. Granny was simply quivering as she watched the wheel. "Can she really imagine that zéro will win again?" I thought, looking at her with wonder. Her face was beaming with a firm conviction of winning, an unhesitating expectation that in another minute they would shout zéro. The ball jumped into the cage.

"Zéro!" cried the croupier.

"What!!!" Granny turned to me with intense triumph.

I was a gambler myself, I felt that at the moment my arms and legs were trembling, there was a throbbing in my head. Of course, this was a rare chance that zéro should have come up three times in some dozen turns; but there was nothing particularly wonderful about it. I had myself seen zéro turn up three times *running* two days before, and a gambler who had been zealously noting down the lucky numbers, observed aloud that, only the day before, zéro had turned up only once in twenty-four hours.

Granny's winnings were counted out to her with particular attention and deference as she had won such a large sum. She received four hundred and twenty friedrichs d'or, that is, four thousand florins and seventy friedrichs d'or. She was given twenty friedrichs d'or in gold, and four thousand florins in banknotes.

This time Granny did not call Potapitch; she had other preoccupations. She did not even babble or quiver outwardly! She was, if one may so express it, quivering inwardly. She was entirely concentrated on something, absorbed in one aim.

"Alexey Ivanovitch, he said that one could only stake four thousand florins at once, didn't he? Come, take it, stake the whole four thousand on the red," Granny commanded.

It was useless to protest; the wheel began rotating.

"*Rouge*," the croupier proclaimed.

Again she had won four thousand florins, making eight in all.

"Give me four, and stake four again on red," Granny commanded.

Again I staked four thousand.

"*Rouge*," the croupier pronounced again.

"Twelve thousand altogether! Give it me all here. Pour the gold here into the purse and put away the notes. That's enough! Home! Wheel my chair out."

CHAPTER XI

THE CHAIR WAS wheeled to the door at the other end of the room. Granny was radiant. All our party immediately thronged round her with congratulations. However eccentric Granny's behaviour might be, her triumph covered a multitude of sins, and the General was no longer afraid of compromising himself in public by his relationship with such a strange woman. With a condescending and familiarly good-humoured smile, as though humouring a child, he congratulated Granny. He was, however, evidently impressed, like all the other spectators. People talked all round and pointed at Granny. Many passed by to get a closer view of her! Mr. Astley was talking of her aside, with two English acquaintances. Some majestic ladies gazed at her with majestic amazement, as though at a marvel . . . De Grieux positively showered congratulations and smiles upon her.

"*Quelle victoire!*" he said.

"*Mais, Madame, c'était du feu,*" Mlle. Blanche commented, with an ingratiating smile.

"Yes, I just went and won twelve thousand florins! Twelve, indeed; what about the gold? With the gold it makes almost thirteen. What is that in our money? Will it be six thousand?"

I explained that it made more than seven, and in the present state of exchange might even amount to eight.

"Well, that's something worth having, eight thousand! And you stay here, you noodles, and do nothing! Potapitch, Marfa, did you see?"

"My goodness! how did you do it, Ma'am? Eight thousand!" exclaimed Marfa, wriggling.

"There! there's five gold pieces for you, here!"

Potapitch and Marfa flew to kiss her hand.

"And give the porters, too, a friedrich d'or each. Give it them in gold, Alexey Ivanovitch. Why is that flunkey bowing and the other one too? Are they congratulating me? Give them a friedrich d'or too."

"*Madame la princesse . . . un pauvre expatrié . . . malheur continuel . . . les princes russes sont si généreux . . .*" A person with moustaches and an obsequious smile, in a threadbare coat and gay-coloured waistcoat, came cringing about Granny's chair, waving his hat in his hand.

"Give him a friedrich d'or too. . . . No, give him two; that's enough, or there will be no end to them. Lift me up and carry me out. Praskovya" — she turned to Polina Alexandrovna, — "I'll buy you a dress to-morrow, and I'll buy Mlle. . . . what's her name, Mlle. Blanche, isn't it? I'll buy her a dress too. Translate that to her, Praskovya!"

"*Merci, Madame.*" Mlle. Blanche made a grateful curtsey while she exchanged an ironical smile with De Grieux and the General. The General was rather embarrassed and was greatly relieved when we reached the avenue.

"Fedosya — won't Fedosya be surprised," said Granny, thinking of the General's nurse. "I must make her a present of a dress. Hey, Alexey Ivanovitch, Alexey Ivanovitch, give this to the poor man."

A man in rags, with bent back, passed us on the road, and looked at us.

"And perhaps he is not a poor man, but a rogue, Granny."

"Give him a gulden, give it him!"

I went up to the man and gave it him. He looked at me in wild amazement, but took the gulden, however. He smelt of spirits.

"And you, Alexey Ivanovitch. Have you not tried your luck yet?"

"No, Granny."

"But your eyes were burning, I saw them."

"I shall try, Granny, I certainly shall later."

"And stake on zéro straight away. You will see! How much have you in hand?"

"Only twenty friedrichs d'or, Granny."

"That's not much. I will give you fifty friedrichs d'or. I will lend it if you like. Here, take this roll — but don't you expect anything, all the same, my good man, I am not going to give you anything," she said, suddenly addressing the General.

The latter winced, but he said nothing. De Grieux frowned.

"*Que diable, c'est une terrible vieille!*" he muttered to the General through his teeth.

"A beggar, a beggar, another beggar!" cried Granny. "Give him a gulden, too, Alexey Ivanovitch."

This time it was a grey-headed old man with a wooden leg, in a long-skirted blue coat and with a long stick in his hand. He looked like an old soldier. But when I held out a gulden to him he stepped back and looked at me angrily.

"*Was ist's der Teufel,*" he shouted, following up with a dozen oaths.

"Oh, he's a fool," cried Granny, dismissing him with a wave of her hand. "Go on! I'm hungry! Now we'll have dinner directly; then I'll rest a little, and back here again."

"You want to play again, Granny!" I cried.

"What do you expect? That you should all sit here and sulk while I watch you?"

"*Mais, madame —*" De Grieux drew near — "*les chances peuvent tourner, une seule mauvaise chance et vous perdrez tout . . . surtout avec votre jeu . . . C'est terrible!*"

"*Vous perdrez absolument*," chirped Mlle. Blanche.

"But what is it to do with all of you? I shouldn't lose your money, but my own! And where is that Mr. Astley?" she asked me.

"He stayed in the Casino, Granny."

"I'm sorry, he's such a nice man."

On reaching home Granny met the *ober-kellner* on the stairs, called him and began bragging of her winnings; then she sent for Fedosya, made her a present of three friedrichs d'or and ordered dinner to be served. Fedosya and Marfa hovered over her at dinner.

"I watched you, ma'am," Marfa cackled, "and said to Potapitch, 'What does our lady want to do?' And the money on the table — saints alive! the money! I haven't seen so much money in the whole of my life, and all round were gentlefolks — nothing but gentlefolks sitting. 'And wherever do all these gentlefolk come from, Potapitch?' said I. May our Lady Herself help her, I thought. I was praying for you, ma'am, and my heart was simply sinking, simply sinking; I was all of a tremble. Lord help her, I thought, and here the Lord has sent you luck. I've been trembling ever since, ma'am. I'm all of a tremble now."

"Alexey Ivanovitch, after dinner, at four o'clock, get ready and we'll go. Now good-bye for a time; don't forget to send for a doctor for me. I must drink the waters, too. Go, or maybe you'll forget."

As I left Granny I was in a sort of stupor. I tried to imagine what would happen now to all our people and what turn things would take. I saw clearly that they (especially the General) had not yet succeeded in recovering from the first shock. The fact of Granny's arrival instead of the telegram which they were expecting from hour to hour to announce her death (and consequently the inheritance of her fortune), had so completely shattered the whole fabric of their plans and intentions, that Granny's further exploits at roulette threw them into positive bewilderment and a sort of stupefaction seemed to have come over all of them.

Meanwhile this second fact was almost more important than the first; for though Granny had repeated twice that she would not give the General any money, yet, who knows? — there was no need to give up all hope yet. De Grieux, who was involved in all the General's affairs, had not lost hope. I am convinced that Mlle. Blanche, also much involved in the General's affairs (I should think so: to marry a General and with a considerable fortune!) would not have given up hope, and would have tried all her fascinating arts upon Granny — in contrast with the proud and incomprehensible Polina, who did not know how to curry favour with any one. But now, now that Granny had had such success at roulette, now that Granny's personality had shown itself so clearly and so typically (a refractory and imperious old lady, *et tombée en enfance*), now, perhaps, all was lost. Why, she was as pleased as a child, so pleased that she would go on till she was ruined and had lost everything. Heavens! I thought (and, God forgive me, with a malignant laugh), why, every friedrich d'or Granny staked just now must have been a fresh sore in the General's heart, must have maddened De Grieux and infuriated Mlle. de Cominges, who saw the cup slipping from her lips. Another fact: even in her triumph and joy of winning, when Granny was giving money away to every one, and taking every passer-by for a beggar, even then she had let fall to the General, "I'm not going to give you anything, though!" That meant that she had fastened upon that idea, was sticking to it, had made up her mind about it. There was danger! danger!

All these reflections were revolving in my mind as I mounted the front stairs from Granny's apartments to my garret in the very top storey. All this interested me strongly. Though, of course, I could before have divined the strongest leading motives prompting the actors before me, yet I did not know for certain all the mysteries and intrigues of the drama. Polina had never been fully open with me. Though it did happen at times that she revealed her feelings to me, yet I noticed that almost always after such confidences she would make fun of all she had said, or would try to obscure the matter and put it in a different light. Oh, she had hidden a great deal! In any case, I foresaw that the *dénouement* of this mysterious and constrained position was at hand. One more shock—and everything would be ended and revealed. About my fortunes, which were also involved in all this, I scarcely troubled. I was in a strange mood: I had only twenty friedrichs d'or in my pocket; I was in a foreign land without a job or means of livelihood, without hope, without prospects, and—I did not trouble my head about it! If it had not been for the thought of Polina, I should have abandoned myself to the comic interest of the approaching catastrophe, and should have been shouting with laughter. But I was troubled about Polina; her fate was being decided, I divined that; but I regret to say that it was not altogether her fate that troubled me. I wanted to fathom her secrets; I wanted her to come to me and say: "I love you," and if not that, if that was senseless insanity, then . . . well, what was there to care about? Did I know what I wanted? I was like one demented: all I wanted was to be near her, in the halo of her glory, in her radiance, always, for ever, all my life. I knew nothing more! And could I leave her?

In their passage on the third storey I felt as though something nudged me. I turned round and, twenty paces or more from me, I saw coming out of a door Polina. She seemed waiting: and as soon as she saw me beckoned to me.

"Polina Alexandrovna . . ."

"Hush!" she said.

"Imagine," I whispered to her, "I felt as though some one had nudged me just now; I looked round — you! It seems as though there were a sort of electricity from you!"

"Take this letter," Polina articulated anxiously with a frown, probably not hearing what I had said, "and give it into Mr. Astley's own hands at once. Make haste, I beg you. There is no need of an answer. He will . . ."

She did not finish.

"Mr. Astley?" I repeated in surprise.

But Polina had already disappeared behind the door.

"Aha, so they are in correspondence!" I ran at once, of course, to Mr. Astley; first to his hotel, where I did not find him, then to the Casino, where I hurried through all the rooms: and at last, as I was returning home in vexation, almost in despair, I met him by chance, with a party of Englishmen and Englishwomen on horseback. I beckoned to him, stopped him and gave him the letter: we had not time even to exchange a glance. But I suspect that Mr. Astley purposely gave rein to his horse.

Was I tortured by jealousy? Anyway, I was in an utterly shattered condition. I did not even want to find out what they were writing to one another about. And so he was trusted by her! "Her friend, her friend," I thought, "and that is clear (and when has he had time to become her friend), but is there love in the case? Of course not," common-sense whispered to me. But common-sense alone counts for little in such cases; anyway, this, too, had to be cleared up. Things were growing unpleasantly complicated.

Before I had time to go into the hotel, first the porter and then the *ober-kellner*, coming out of his room, informed me that I was wanted, that I had been asked for, three times they had sent to ask: where was I? — that I was asked to go as quickly as possible to the General's rooms. I was in the most disagreeable frame of mind. In the General's room I found, besides the General himself, De Grieux and Mlle. Blanche — alone, without her mother. The mother was evidently an official one, only used for show. But when it came to real *business* she acted for herself. And probably the woman knew little of her so-called daughter's affairs.

They were, however, consulting warmly about something, and the doors of the study were actually locked — which had never happened before. Coming to the door, I heard loud voices — De Grieux's insolent and malignant voice, Blanche's shrill fury, and the General's pitiful tones, evidently defending himself about something. Upon my entrance they all, as it were, pulled themselves up and restrained themselves. De

Grieux smoothed his hair and forced a smile into his angry face — that horrid official French smile which I so detest. The crushed and desperate General tried to assume an air of dignity, but it was a mechanical effort. Only Mlle. Blanche's countenance, blazing with anger, scarcely changed. She only ceased speaking while she fixed her eyes upon me in impatient expectation. I may mention that hitherto she had treated me with extraordinary casualness, had even refused to respond to my bows, and had simply declined to see me.

"Alexey Ivanovitch," the General began in a soft and mollifying tone; "allow me to tell you that it is strange, exceedingly strange . . . in fact, your conduct in regard to me and my family . . . in fact, it is exceedingly strange . . ."

• "*Eh! ce n'est pas ça,*" De Grieux interposed, with vexation and contempt. (There's no doubt he was the leading spirit.) "*Mon cher monsieur, notre cher général se trompe,* in taking up this tone" (I translate the rest of his speech in Russian), "but he meant to say . . . that is to warn you, or rather to beg you most earnestly not to ruin him — yes, indeed, not to ruin him! I make use of that expression."

"But how, how?" I interrupted.

"Why, you are undertaking to be the guide (or how shall I express it?) of this old woman, *cette pauvre terrible vieille*" — De Grieux himself hesitated — "but you know she'll lose everything; she will gamble away her whole fortune! You know yourself, you have seen yourself, how she plays! If she begins to lose, she will never leave off from obstinacy, from anger, and will lose everything, she will gamble away everything, and in such cases one can never regain one's losses and then . . . then . . ."

"And then," the General put in, "then you will ruin the whole family! I and my family are her heirs, she has no nearer relations. I tell you openly: my affairs are in a bad way, a very bad way. You know my position to some extent . . . If she loses a considerable sum or even (Lord help us!) her whole fortune, what will become of me, of my children!" (The General looked round at De Grieux.) "Of me." (He looked round at Mlle. Blanche, who turned away from him with contempt.) "Alexey Ivanovitch, save us, save us! . . ."

"But how, General, how, how can I? . . . What influence have I in the matter?"

"Refuse, refuse, give her up! . . ."

"Then some one else will turn up," I said.

"*Ce n'est pas ça, ce n'est pas ça,*" De Grieux interrupted again, "*que diable!* No, don't desert her, but at least advise her, dissuade her, draw her away . . . don't let her play too much, distract her in some way."

"But how can I do that? If you would undertake the task yourself, M. de Grieux," I added, as naïvely as I could.

Here I caught a rapid, fiery, questioning glance from Mlle. Blanche at M. de Grieux. And in De Grieux's own face there was something peculiar, something he could not himself disguise.

"The point is, she won't accept me now!" De Grieux cried, with a wave of his hand. "If only . . . later on . . ."

De Grieux looked rapidly and meaningly at Mlle. Blanche.

"*O, mon cher M. Alexis, soyez si bon.*" Mlle. Blanche herself took a step towards me with a most fascinating smile, she seized me by both hands and pressed them warmly. Damn it all! That diabolical face knew how to change completely in one moment. At that instant her face was so imploring, so sweet, it was such a child-like and even mischievous smile; at the end of the phrase she gave me such a sly wink, unseen by all the rest; she meant to do for me completely, and it was successfully done; only it was horribly coarse.

Then the General leapt up, positively leapt up. "Alexey Ivanovitch, forgive me for beginning as I did just now. I did not mean that at all. . . . I beg you, I beseech you, I bow down before you in Russian style—you alone, you alone can save us. Mlle. de Cominges and I implore you—you understand, you understand, of course." He besought me, indicating Mlle. Blanche with his eyes. He was a very pitiful figure.

At that instant there came three subdued and respectful knocks at the door; it was opened—the corridor attendant was knocking and a few steps behind him stood Potapitch. They came with messages from Granny; they were charged to find and bring me at once. "She is angry," Potapitch informed me.

"But it is only half-past three."

"She could not get to sleep; she kept tossing about, and then at last she got up, sent for her chair and for you. She's at the front door now."

"*Quelle mégère,*" cried De Grieux.

I did, in fact, find Granny on the steps, out of all patience at my not being there. She could not wait till four o'clock.

"Come," she cried, and we set off again to roulette.

CHAPTER XII

GRANNY WAS IN an impatient and irritable mood; it was evident that roulette had made a deep impression on her mind. She took no notice of anything else and was altogether absent-minded. For instance, she asked me no questions on the road as she had done before. Seeing a luxurious carriage whirling by, she was on the point of raising her hand and asking: What is it? Whose is it? — but I believe she did not hear what I answered: her absorption was continually interrupted by abrupt and impatient gesticulations. When I pointed out to her Baron and Baroness Burmerhelm, who were approaching the Casino, she looked absent-mindedly at them and said, quite indifferently, "Ah!" and, turning round quickly to Potapitch and Marfa, who were walking behind her, snapped out to them —

"Why are you hanging upon us? We can't take you every time! Go home! You and I are enough," she added, when they had hurriedly turned and gone home.

They were already expecting Granny at the Casino. They immediately made room for her in the same place, next to the croupier. I fancy that these croupiers, who are always so strictly decorous and appear to be ordinary officials who are absolutely indifferent as to whether the bank wins or loses, are by no means so unconcerned at the bank's losses and, of course, receive instructions for attracting players and for augmenting the profits — for which they doubtless receive prizes and bonuses. They looked upon Granny, anyway, as their prey.

Then just what we had expected happened.

This was how it was.

Granny pounced at once on zéro and immediately ordered me to stake twelve friedrichs d'or. She staked once, twice, three times — zéro never turned up.

"Put it down! Put it down!" Granny nudged me, impatiently. I obeyed.

"How many times have we staked?" she asked at last, grinding her teeth with impatience.

"I have staked twelve times, Granny. I have put down a hundred and forty-four friedrichs d'or. I tell you, Granny, very likely till evening . . ."

"Hold your tongue!" Granny interrupted. "Stake on zéro, and stake at once a thousand guldens on red. Here, take the note."

Red won, and zéro failed once more; a thousand guldens was gained.

"You see, you see!" whispered Granny, "we have gained almost all that we have lost. Stake again on zéro; we'll stake ten times more and then give it up."

But the fifth time Granny was thoroughly sick of it.

"The devil take that filthy zéro. Come, stake the whole four thousand guldens on the red," she commanded me.

"Granny! it will be so much; why, what if red does not turn up?" I besought her; but Granny almost beat me. (Indeed, she nudged me so violently that she might almost be said to have attacked me.) There was no help for it, I staked on red the whole four thousand won that morning. The wheel turned. Granny sat calmly and proudly erect, never doubting that she would certainly win.

"Zéro!" boomed the croupier.

At first Granny did not understand, but when she saw the croupier scoop up her four thousand guldens together with everything on the table, and learned that zéro, which had not turned up for so long and on which we had staked in vain almost two hundred friedrichs d'or, had, as though to spite her, turned up just as Granny was abusing it, she groaned and flung up her hands in view of the whole hall. People around actually laughed.

"Holy saints! The cursed thing has turned up!" Granny wailed; "the hateful, hateful thing! That's your doing! It's all your doing" — she pounced upon me furiously, pushing me. "It was you persuaded me."

"Granny, I talked sense to you; how can I answer for chance?"

"I'll chance you," she whispered angrily. "Go away."

"Good-bye, Granny." I turned to go away.

"Alexey Ivanovitch, Alexey Ivanovitch! stop. Where are you off to? Come, what's the matter, what's the matter? Ach, he's in a rage! Stupid, come, stay, stay; come, don't be angry; I am a fool myself! Come, tell me what are we to do now!"

"I won't undertake to tell you, Granny, because you will blame me. Play for yourself, tell me and I'll put down the stakes."

"Well, well! Come, stake another four thousand guldens on red! Here, take my pocket-book." She took it out of her pocket and gave it me. "Come, make haste and take it, there's twenty thousand roubles sterling in it."

"Granny," I murmured, "such stakes . . ."

"As sure as I am alive, I'll win it back. . . . Stake."

We staked and lost.

"Stake, stake the whole eight!"

"You can't, Granny, four is the highest stake! . . ."

"Well, stake four!"

This time we won. Granny cheered up.

"You see, you see," she nudged me; "stake four again!"

She staked — she lost; then we lost again and again.

"Granny, the whole twelve thousand is gone," I told her.

"I see it's all gone," she answered with the calm of fury, if I may so express it. "I see, my good friend, I see," she muttered, with a fixed, as it were, absent-minded stare. "Ech, as sure as I am alive, stake another four thousand guldens!"

"But there's no money, Granny; there are some of our Russian five per cents. and some bills of exchange of some sort, but no money."

"And in the purse?"

"There's some small change, Granny."

"Are there any money-changers here? I was told one could change any of our notes," Granny inquired resolutely.

"Oh, as much as you like, but what you'll lose on the exchange . . . would horrify a Jew!"

"Nonsense! I'll win it all back. Take me! Call those blockheads!"

I wheeled away the chair; the porters appeared and we went out of the Casino.

"Make haste, make haste, make haste," Granny commanded. "Show us the way, Alexey Ivanovitch, and take us the nearest . . . Is it far?"

"Two steps, Granny."

But at the turning from the square into the avenue we were met by our whole party: the General, De Grieux, Mlle. Blanche and her Mamma. Polina Alexandrovna was not with them, nor Mr. Astley either.

"Well! Don't stop us!" cried Granny. "Well, what do you want? I have no time to spare for you now!"

I walked behind; De Grieux ran up to me.

"She's lost all she gained this morning and twelve thousand guldens as well. We are going to change some five per cents.," I whispered to him quickly.

De Grieux stamped and ran to tell the General. We went on wheeling Granny.

"Stop, stop!" the General whispered to me frantically.

"You try stopping her," I whispered.

"Auntie!" said the General, approaching, "Auntie . . . we are just . . . we are just . . ." his voice quivered and failed him, "hiring a horse and driving into the country . . . a most exquisite view . . . the peak . . . We were coming to invite you."

"Oh, bother you and your peak." Granny waved him off irritably.

"There are trees there . . . we will have tea . . ." the General went on, utterly desperate.

"*Nous boirons du lait, sur l'herbe fraîche,*" added De Grieux, with ferocious fury.

Du lait, de l'herbe fraîche, that is the Paris bourgeois notion of the ideally idyllic; that is, as we all know, his conception of *nature et la vérité!*

"Oh, go on with you and your milk! Lap it up yourself; it gives me the bellyache. And why do you pester me?" cried Granny. "I tell you I've no time to waste."

"It's here, Granny," I said; "it's here!"

We had reached the house where the bank was. I went in to change

the notes; Granny was left waiting at the entrance; De Grieux, the
General and Blanche stood apart waiting, not knowing what to do.
Granny looked wrathfully at them, and they walked away in the direc-
tion of the Casino.

They offered me such ruinous terms that I did not accept them, and
went back to Granny for instructions.

"Ah, the brigands!" she cried, flinging up her hands. "Well, never
mind! Change it," she cried resolutely; "stay, call the banker out
to me!"

"One of the clerks, Granny, do you mean?"

"Yes, a clerk, it's all the same. Ach, the brigands!"

The clerk consented to come when he learned that it was an invalid
and aged countess, unable to come in, who was asking for him. Granny
spent a long time loudly and angrily reproaching him for swindling her,
and haggled with him in a mixture of Russian, French and German,
while I came to the rescue in translating. The grave clerk listened to us
in silence and shook his head. He looked at Granny with an intent stare
that was hardly respectful; at last he began smiling.

"Well, get along with you," cried Granny. "Choke yourself with the
money! Change it with him, Alexey Ivanovitch; there's no time to waste,
or we would go elsewhere. . . ."

"The clerk says that other banks give even less."

I don't remember the sums exactly, but the banker's charges were
terrible. I received close upon twelve thousand florins in gold and notes,
took the account and carried it to Granny.

"Well, well, well, it's no use counting it," she said, with a wave of her
hand. "Make haste, make haste, make haste!"

"I'll never stake again on that damned zéro nor on the red either," she
pronounced, as she was wheeled up to the Casino.

This time I did my very utmost to impress upon her the necessity of
staking smaller sums, trying to persuade her that with the change of luck
she would always be able to increase her stake. But she was so impatient
that, though she agreed at first, it was impossible to restrain her when the
play had begun; as soon as she had won a stake of ten, of twenty
friedrichs d'or ——

"There, you see, there, you see," she would begin nudging me; "there,
you see, we've won; if only we had staked four thousand instead of ten,
we should have won four thousand, but as it is what's the good? It's all
your doing, all your doing!"

And, vexed as I felt, watching her play, I made up my mind at last to
keep quiet and to give no more advice.

Suddenly De Grieux skipped up.

The other two were close by; I noticed Mlle. Blanche standing on one side with her mother, exchanging amenities with the Prince. The General was obviously out of favour, almost banished. Blanche would not even look at him, though he was doing his utmost to cajole her! The poor General! He flushed and grew pale by turns, trembled and could not even follow Granny's play. Blanche and the Prince finally went away; the General ran after them.

"Madame, madame," De Grieux whispered in a honeyed voice to Granny, squeezing his way close up to her ear. "Madame, such stakes do not answer. . . . No, no, it's impossible . . ." he said, in broken Russian. "No!"

"How, then? Come, show me!" said Granny, turning to him.

De Grieux babbled something rapidly in French, began excitedly advising, said she must wait for a chance, began reckoning some numbers. . . . Granny did not understand a word. He kept turning to me, for me to translate; tapped the table with his fingers, pointed; finally took a pencil and was about to reckon something on paper. At last Granny lost patience.

"Come, get away, get away! You keep talking nonsense! 'Madame, madame,' he doesn't understand it himself; go away."

"*Mais, madame*," De Grieux murmured, and he began once more showing and explaining.

"Well, stake once as he says," Granny said to me; "let us see: perhaps it really will answer."

All De Grieux wanted was to dissuade her from staking large sums; he suggested that she should stake on numbers, either individually or collectively. I staked as he directed, a friedrich d'or on each of the odd numbers in the first twelve and five friedrichs d'or respectively on the groups of numbers from twelve to eighteen and from eighteen to twenty-four, staking in all sixteen friedrichs d'or.

The wheel turned.

"Zéro," cried the croupier.

We had lost everything.

"You blockhead!" cried Granny, addressing De Grieux. "You scoundrelly Frenchman! So this is how he advises, the monster. Go away, go away! He knows nothing about it and comes fussing round!"

Fearfully offended, De Grieux shrugged his shoulders, looked contemptuously at Granny, and walked away. He felt ashamed of having interfered; he had been in too great a hurry.

An hour later, in spite of all our efforts, we had lost everything.

"Home," cried Granny.

She did not utter a single word till we got into the avenue. In the

avenue and approaching the hotel she began to break into ex-
clamations —

"What a fool! What a silly fool! You're an old fool, you are!"

As soon as we got to her apartments —

"Tea!" cried Granny. "And pack up at once! We are going!"

"Where does your honour mean to go?" Marfa was beginning.

"What is it to do with you? Mind your own business! Potapitch, pack
up everything: all the luggage. We are going back to Moscow. I have
thrown away fifteen thousand roubles!"

"Fifteen thousand, madame! My God!" Potapitch cried, flinging up
his hands with deep feeling, probably meaning to humour her.

"Come, come, you fool! He is beginning to whimper! Hold your
tongue! Pack up! The bill, make haste, make haste!"

"The next train goes at half-past nine, Granny," I said, to check her
furore.

"And what is it now?"

"Half-past seven."

"How annoying! Well, it doesn't matter! Alexey Ivanovitch, I haven't a
farthing. Here are two more notes. Run there and change these for me
too. Or I have nothing for the journey."

I set off. Returning to the hotel half an hour later, I found our whole
party at Granny's. Learning that Granny was going off to Moscow, they
seemed to be even more upset than by her losses. Even though her going
might save her property, what was to become of the General? Who
would pay De Grieux? Mlle. Blanche would, of course, decline to wait
for Granny to die and would certainly now make up to the Prince or to
somebody else. They were all standing before Granny, trying to console
her and persuade her. Again Polina was not there. Granny was shouting
at them furiously.

"Let me alone, you devils! What business is it of yours? Why does that
goat's beard come forcing himself upon me?" she cried at De Grieux;
"and you, my fine bird?" she cried, addressing Mlle. Blanche, "what are
you after?"

"*Diantre!*" whispered Mlle. Blanche, with an angry flash of her eyes,
but suddenly she burst out laughing and went out of the room.

"*Elle vivra cent ans!*" she called to the General, as she went out of the
door.

"Ah, so you are reckoning on my death?" Granny yelled to the
General. "Get away! Turn them all out, Alexey Ivanovitch! What business is it of yours? I've fooled away my own money, not yours!"

The General shrugged his shoulders, bowed and went out. De Grieux
followed him.

"Call Praskovya," Granny told Marfa.

Five minutes later Marfa returned with Polina. All this time Polina had been sitting in her own room with the children, and I fancy had purposely made up her mind not to go out all day. Her face was serious, sad and anxious.

"Praskovya," began Granny, "is it true, as I learned by accident just now, that that fool, your stepfather, means to marry that silly feather-head of a Frenchwoman — an actress is she, or, something worse? Tell me, is it true?"

"I don't know anything about it for certain, Granny," answered Polina, "but from the words of Mlle. Blanche herself, who does not feel it necessary to conceal anything, I conclude . . ."

"Enough," Granny broke in vigorously, "I understand! I always reckoned that he was capable of it and I have always thought him a most foolish and feather-headed man. He thinks no end of himself, because he is a General (he was promoted from a Colonel on retiring), and he gives himself airs. I know, my good girl, how you kept sending telegram after telegram to Moscow, to ask if your old Granny would soon be laid out. They were on the look-out for my money; without money that nasty hussy, what's her name — de Cominges — wouldn't take him for her footman, especially with his false teeth. She has a lot of money herself, they say, lends at interest, has made a lot. I am not blaming you, Praskovya, it wasn't you who sent the telegrams; and I don't want to remember the past, either. I know you've got a bad temper — a wasp! You can sting to hurt; but I'm sorry for you because I was fond of your mother, Katerina. Well, you throw up everything here and come with me. You've nowhere to go, you know; and it's not fitting for you to be with them now. Stop!" cried Granny, as Polina was about to speak; "I've not finished. I ask nothing of you. As you know, I have in Moscow a palace; you can have a whole storey to yourself and not come and see me for weeks at a time if my temper does not suit you! Well, will you or not?"

"Let me ask you first: do you really mean to set off at once?"

"Do you suppose I'm joking, my good girl! I've said I'm going and I'm going. I've wasted fifteen thousand roubles to-day over your damned roulette. Five years ago I promised to rebuild a wooden church with stone on my estate near Moscow, and instead of that I've thrown away my money here. Now, my girl, I'm going home to build the church."

"And the waters, Granny? You came to drink the waters?"

"Bother you and the waters, too. Don't irritate me, Praskovya; are you doing it on purpose? Tell me, will you come or not?"

"I thank you very, very much," Polina began, with feeling, "for the home you offer me. You have guessed my position to some extent. I am so grateful to you that I shall perhaps come to you soon; but now there are reasons . . . important reasons . . . and I can't decide at once, on the spur of the moment. If you were staying only a fortnight . . ."

"You mean you won't?"

"I mean I can't. Besides, in any case I can't leave my brother and sister, as . . . as . . . as it may actually happen that they may be left abandoned, so . . . if you would take me with the children, Granny, I certainly would come, and, believe me, I would repay you for it!" she added warmly; "but without the children I can't come, Granny."

"Well, don't whimper" (Polina had no intention of whimpering — indeed, I had never seen her cry). "Some place will be found for the chickens, my henhouse is big enough. Besides, it is time they were at school. Well, so you are not coming now! Well, Praskovya, mind! I wished for your good, but I know why you won't come! I know all about it, Praskovya. That Frenchman will bring you no good."

Polina flushed crimson. I positively shuddered. (Every one knows all about it. I am the only one to know nothing!)

"Come, come, don't frown. I am not going to say anything more. Only take care no harm comes of it, understand. You are a clever wench; I shall be sorry for you. Well, that's enough. I should not like to look on you as on the others! Go along, good-bye!"

"I'll come to see you off," said Polina.

"There's no need, don't you interfere; I am sick of you all."

Polina was kissing Granny's hand, but the latter pulled it away and kissed her on the cheek.

As she passed me, Polina looked at me quickly and immediately turned away her eyes.

"Well, good-bye to you, too, Alexey Ivanovitch, there's only an hour before the train starts, and I think you must be tired out with me. Here, take these fifty pieces of gold."

"I thank you very much, Granny; I'm ashamed . . ."

"Come, come!" cried Granny, but so vigorously and angrily that I dared say no more and took it.

"When you are running about Moscow without a job come to me: I will give you some introductions. Now, get along with you!"

I went to my room and lay down on my bed. I lay there for half an hour on my back, with my hands clasped behind my head. The catastrophe had come at last, I had something to think about. I made up my mind to talk earnestly to Polina. The nasty Frenchman! So it was true then! But what could there be at the bottom of it? Polina and De Grieux! Heavens! what a pair!

It was all simply incredible. I suddenly jumped up, beside myself, to look for Mr. Astley, and at all costs to make him speak out. No doubt in this matter, too, he knew more than I did. Mr. Astley? He was another riddle to me!

But suddenly there was a tap at my door. I looked up. It was Potapitch.

"Alexey Ivanovitch, you are wanted to come to my lady!"

"What's the matter? Is she setting off? The train does not start for twenty minutes."

"She's uneasy, she can't sit still. 'Make haste, make haste!' she says, meaning to fetch you, sir. For Christ's sake, don't delay."

I ran downstairs at once. Granny was being wheeled out into the passage, her pocket-book was in her hand.

"Alexey Ivanovitch, go on ahead; we're coming."

"Where, Granny?"

"As sure as I'm alive, I'll win it back. Come, march, don't ask questions! Does the play go on there till midnight?"

I was thunderstruck. I thought a moment, but at once made up my mind.

"Do as you please, Antonida Vassilyevna, I'm not coming."

"What's that for? What now? Have you all eaten too many pancakes, or what?"

"Do as you please, I should blame myself for it afterwards; I won't. I won't take part in it or look on at it; spare me, Antonida Vassilyevna. Here are your fifty friedrichs d'or back; good-bye!" And, laying the fifty friedrichs d'or on the little table near which Granny's chair was standing, I bowed and went out.

"What nonsense!" Granny shouted after me. "Don't come if you don't want to, I can find the way by myself! Potapitch, come with me! Come, lift me up, carry me!"

I did not find Mr. Astley and returned home. It was late, after midnight, when I learned from Potapitch how Granny's day ended. She lost all that I had changed for her that evening—that is, in Russian money, another ten thousand roubles. The little Pole, to whom she had given two friedrichs d'or the day before, had attached himself to her and had directed her play the whole time. At first, before the Pole came, she had made Potapitch put down the stakes, but soon she dismissed him; it was at that moment the Pole turned up. As ill-luck would have it, he understood Russian and babbled away in a mixture of three languages, so that they understood each other after a fashion. Granny abused him mercilessly the whole time; and though he incessantly "laid himself at his lady's feet," "yet he couldn't be compared with you, Alexey Ivanovitch," said Potapitch. "She treated you *like a gentleman*, while the other—I saw it with my own eyes, God strike me dead—stole her money off the table. She caught him at it herself twice. She did give it to him with all sorts of names, sir, even pulled his hair once, upon my word she did, so that folks were laughing round about. She's lost everything, sir, everything, all you changed for her; we brought her back here — she only asked for a drink of water, crossed herself and went to bed. She's worn out, to be sure; she fell asleep at once. God send her heavenly dreams. Och! these foreign parts!" Potapitch wound up. "I said it would lead to no good. If only we could soon be back in Moscow! We'd everything we wanted at home in Moscow: a garden, flowers such as you don't have here, fragrance, the apples are swelling, plenty of room everywhere. No, we had to come abroad. Oh, oh, oh . . ."

CHAPTER XIII

NOW ALMOST A whole month has passed since I touched these notes of mine, which were begun under the influence of confused but intense impressions. The catastrophe which I felt to be approaching has actually come, but in a form a hundred times more violent and startling than I had expected. It has all been something strange, grotesque and even tragic — at least for me. Several things have happened to me that were almost miraculous; that is, at least, how I look upon them to this day — though from another point of view, particularly in the whirl of events in which I was involved at that time, they were only somewhat out of the common. But what is most marvellous to me is my own attitude to all these events. To this day I cannot understand myself, and it has all floated by like a dream — even my passion — it was violent and sincere, but . . . what has become of it now? It is true that sometimes the thought flashes through my brain: "Wasn't I out of my mind then, and wasn't I all that time somewhere in a madhouse and perhaps I'm there now, so that was all my fancy and still is my fancy . . ." I put my notes together and read them over. (Who knows — perhaps to convince myself that I did not write them in a madhouse.) Now I am entirely alone. Autumn is coming on and the leaves are turning yellow. I'm still in this dismal little town (oh! how dismal the little German towns are!), and instead of considering what to do next, I go on living under the influence of the sensations I have just passed through, under the influence of memories still fresh, under the influence of the whirl of events which caught me up and flung me aside again. At times I fancy that I am still caught up in that whirlwind, that that storm is still raging, carrying me along with it, and again I lose sight of all order and measure and I whirl round and round again. . . .

However, I may, perhaps, leave off whirling and settle down in a way if, so far as I can, I put clearly before my mind all the incidents of the past month. I feel drawn to my pen again. Besides, I have sometimes nothing at all to do in the evenings. I am so hard up for something to do that, odd as it seems, I even take from the scurvy lending library here the novels of Paul de Kock (in a German translation), though I can't endure them; yet I read them and wonder at myself. It is as though I were afraid of breaking the spell of the recent past by a serious book or any serious occupation. It is as though that grotesque dream, and all the impressions left by it, was so precious to me that I am afraid to let anything new touch upon it for fear it should all vanish in smoke. Is it all so precious to me? Yes, of course it is precious. Perhaps I shall remember it for forty years . . .

And so I take up my writing again. I can give a brief account of it to some extent now: the impressions are not at all the same.

In the first place, to finish with Granny. The following day she lost everything. It was what was bound to happen. When once any one is started upon that road, it is like a man in a sledge flying down a snow mountain more and more swiftly. She played all day till eight o'clock in the evening; I was not present and only know what happened from what I was told.

Potapitch was in attendance on her at the Casino all day. Several Poles in succession guided Granny's operations in the course of the day. She began by dismissing the Pole whose hair she had pulled the day before and taking on another, but he turned out almost worse. After dismissing the second, and accepting again the first, who had never left her side, but had been squeezing himself in behind her chair and continually poking his head in during the whole period of his disgrace, she sank at last into complete despair. The second Pole also refused to move away; one stationed himself on her right and the other on her left. They were abusing one another the whole time and quarrelling over the stakes and the game, calling each other "*laidak*" and other Polish civilities, making it up again, putting down money recklessly and playing at random. When they quarrelled they put the money down regardless of each other — one, for instance, on the red and the other on the black. It ended in their completely bewildering and overwhelming Granny, so that at last, almost in tears, she appealed to the old croupier, begging him to protect her and to send them away. They were, in fact, immediately turned out in spite of their outcries and protests; they both shouted out at once and tried to prove that Granny owed them something, that she had deceived them about something and had treated them basely and dishonourably. The luckless Potapitch told me all this the same evening almost with tears, and complained that they stuffed their pockets with money, that he himself had seen them shamelessly steal and continually thrust the money in their pockets. One, for instance, would beg five friedrichs d'or for his trouble and begin putting them down on the spot side by side with Granny's stakes. Granny won, but the man shouted that his stake was the winning one and that Granny's had lost. When they were dismissed Potapitch came forward and said that their pockets were full of gold. Granny at once bade the croupier to look into it and, in spite of the outcries of the Poles (they cackled like two cocks caught in the hand), the police came forward and their pockets were immediately emptied for Granny's benefit. Granny enjoyed unmistakable prestige among the croupiers and the whole staff of the Casino all that day, until she had lost everything. By degrees her fame spread all over the town. All the visitors at the watering-place, of all nations, small and great, streamed to look on at "*une vieille comtesse russe tombée en enfance,*" who had already lost "some millions."

But Granny gained very, very little by being rescued from the two Poles. They were at once replaced by a third, who spoke perfectly pure Russian and was dressed like a gentleman, though he did look like a flunkey with a huge moustache and a sense of his own importance. He, too, "laid himself at his lady's feet and kissed them," but behaved haughtily to those about him, was despotic over the play; in fact, immediately behaved like Granny's master rather than her servant. Every minute, at every turn in the game, he turned to her and swore with awful oaths that he was himself a "*pan* of good position," and that he wouldn't take a kopeck of Granny's money. He repeated this oath so many times that Granny was completely intimidated. But as this *pan* certainly seemed at first to improve her luck, Granny was not willing to abandon him on her own account. An hour later the two Poles who had been turned out of the Casino turned up behind Granny's chair again, and again proffered their services if only to run errands for her. Potapitch swore that the "*pan* of good position" winked at them and even put something in their hands. As Granny had no dinner and could not leave her chair, one of the Poles certainly was of use: he ran off once to the dining-room of the Casino and brought her a cup of broth and afterwards some tea. They both ran about, however. But towards the end of the day, when it became evident to every one that she would stake her last banknote, there were behind her chair as many as six Poles who had never been seen or heard of before. When Granny was playing her last coin, they not only ceased to obey her, but took no notice of her whatever, squeezed their way up to the table in front of her, snatched the money themselves, put down the stakes and made their own play, shouted and quarrelled, talked to the "*pan* of good position" as to one of themselves, while the "*pan* of good position" himself seemed almost oblivious of Granny's existence. Even when Granny, after losing everything, was returning after eight o'clock to the hotel, three or four Poles ran at the side of her bath-chair, still unable to bring themselves to leave her; they kept shouting at the top of their voices, declaring in a hurried gabble that Granny had cheated them in some way and must give them something. They followed her in this way right up to the hotel, from which they were at last driven away with blows.

By Potapitch's reckoning Granny had lost in all ninety thousand roubles that day, apart from what she had lost the day before. All her notes, her exchequer bonds, all the shares she had with her, she had changed, one after another. I marvelled how she could have stood those seven or eight hours sitting there in her chair and scarcely leaving the table, but Potapitch told me that three or four times she had begun winning considerably; and, carried on by fresh hope, she could not tear herself away. But gamblers know how a man can sit for almost twenty-four hours at cards, without looking to right or to left.

Meanwhile, very critical events were taking place all that day at the hotel. In the morning, before eleven o'clock, when Granny was still at home, our people — that is, the General and De Grieux — made up their minds to take the final step. Learning that Granny had given up all idea of setting off, but was going back to the Casino, they went in full conclave (all but Polina) to talk things over with her finally and even *openly*. The General, trembling and with a sinking heart in view of the awful possibilities for himself, overdid it. After spending half an hour in prayers and entreaties and making a clean breast of everything — that is, of all his debts and even his passion for Mlle. Blanche (he quite lost his head), the General suddenly adopted a menacing tone and even began shouting and stamping at Granny; cried that she was disgracing their name, had become a scandal to the whole town, and finally . . . finally: "You are shaming the Russian name," cried the General, and he told her that the police would be called in! Granny finally drove him from her with a stick (an actual stick). The General and De Grieux consulted once or twice that morning, and the question that agitated them was whether it were not possible in some way to bring in the police, on the plea that an unfortunate but venerable old lady, sinking into her dotage, was gambling away her whole fortune, and so on; whether, in fact, it would be possible to put her under any sort of supervision or restraint. . . . But De Grieux only shrugged his shoulders and laughed in the General's face, as the latter pranced up and down his study talking excitedly. Finally, De Grieux went off with a wave of his hand. In the evening we learned that he had left the hotel altogether, after having been in very earnest and mysterious confabulation with Mlle. Blanche. As for Mlle. Blanche, she had taken her measures early in the morning: she threw the General over completely and would not even admit him to her presence. When the General ran to the Casino in search of her and met her arm-in-arm with the Prince, neither she nor Madame de Cominges deigned to notice him. The Prince did not bow to him either. Mlle. Blanche spent that whole day hard at work upon the Prince, trying to force from him a definite declaration. But alas! she was cruelly deceived in her reckoning! This little catastrophe took place in the evening. It suddenly came out that he was as poor as a church mouse, and, what is more, was himself reckoning on borrowing from her on an I O U to try his luck at roulette. Blanche turned him out indignantly and locked herself up in her room.

On the morning of that day I went to Mr. Astley — or, to be more exact, I went in search of Mr. Astley, but could find him nowhere. He was not at home, or in the park, or in the Casino. He was not dining at his hotel that day. It was past four o'clock when I suddenly saw him walking from the railway station towards the Hôtel d'Angleterre. He was in a hurry and was very much preoccupied, though it was hard to trace any anxiety or any perturbation whatever in his face. He held out his hand to me cordially, with his habitual exclamation: "Ah!" but without stopping walked on with rather a rapid step. I attached myself to him, but he managed to answer me in such a way that I did not succeed in even asking him about anything. Moreover, I felt, for some reason, ashamed to begin speaking of Polina; he did not ask a word about her. I told him about Granny. He listened attentively and seriously and shrugged his shoulders.

"She will gamble away everything," I observed.

"Oh, yes," he answered; "she went in to play just as I was going away, and afterwards I learnt for a fact that she had lost everything. If there were time I would look in at the Casino, for it is curious."

"Where have you been?" I cried, wondering that I had not asked before.

"I've been in Frankfurt."

"On business?"

"Yes, on business."

Well, what more was there for me to ask? I did, however, continue walking beside him, but he suddenly turned into the Hôtel des Quatre Saisons, nodded to me and vanished. As I walked home I gradually realized that if I had talked to him for a couple of hours I should have learnt absolutely nothing, because . . . I had nothing to ask him! Yes, that was so, of course! I could not possibly formulate my question.

All that day Polina spent walking with the children and their nurse in the park, or sitting at home. She had for a long time past avoided the General, and scarcely spoke to him about anything — about anything serious, at any rate. I had noticed that for a long time past. But knowing what a position the General was in to-day, I imagined that he could hardly pass her over — that is, there could not but be an important conversation about family affairs between them. When, however, I returned to the hotel, after my conversation with Mr. Astley, I met Polina with the children. There was an expression of the most unruffled calm on her face, as though she alone had remained untouched by the family tempest. She nodded in response to my bow. I returned home feeling quite malignant.

I had, of course, avoided seeing her and had seen nothing of her since the incident with the Burmerhelms. There was some affectation and pose in this; but as time went on, I felt more and more genuinely indignant. Even if she did not care for me in the least, she should not, I thought, have trampled on my feelings like that and have received my declarations so contemptuously. She knew that I really loved her; she admitted me, she allowed me to speak like that! It is true that it had begun rather strangely. Some time before, long ago, in fact, two months before, I began to notice that she wanted to make me her friend, her *confidant*, and indeed was in a way testing me. But somehow this did not come off then; instead of that there remained the strange relations that existed between us; that is how it was I began to speak to her like that. But if my love repelled her, why did she not directly forbid me to speak of it?

She did not forbid me; indeed she sometimes provoked me to talk of it and . . . and, of course, she did this for fun. I know for certain. I noticed it unmistakably — it was agreeable to her to listen and to work me up to a state of misery, to wound me by some display of the utmost contempt and disregard. And, of course, she knew that I could not exist without her. It was three days since the affair with the Baron and I could not endure our separation any longer. When I met her just now near the Casino, my heart throbbed so that I turned pale. But she could not get on without me, either! She needed me and — surely, surely not as a buffoon, a clown?

She had a secret — that was clear! Her conversation with Granny had stabbed my heart. Why, I had urged her a thousand times to be open with me, and she knew that I was ready to give my life for her. But she had always put me off, almost with contempt, or had asked of me, instead of the sacrifice of my life, such pranks as the one with the Baron!

Was not that enough to make one indignant? Could that Frenchman be all the world to her? And Mr. Astley? But at that point the position became utterly incomprehensible — and meanwhile, my God! what agonies I went through!

On getting home, in an access of fury I snatched up my pen and scribbled the following letter to her —

"Polina Alexandrovna, I see clearly that the *dénouement* is at hand which will affect you also. I repeat for the last time: do you need my life or not? If I can be of use in *any way whatever*, dispose of me as you think fit, and I will meanwhile remain in my room and not go out at all. If you need me, write to me or send for me."

I sealed up this note and sent it off by the corridor attendant, instructing him to give it into her hands. I expected no answer, but three minutes later the attendant returned with the message that "she sent her greetings."

It was past six when I was summoned to the General.

He was in his study, dressed as though he were on the point of going out. His hat and coat were lying on the sofa. It seemed to me as I went in that he was standing in the middle of the room with his legs wide apart and his head hanging, talking aloud to himself. But as soon as he saw me, he rushed at me almost crying out, so that I involuntarily stepped back and was almost running away, but he seized me by both hands and drew me to the sofa; sat down on the sofa himself, made me sit down in an armchair just opposite himself, and, keeping tight hold of my hand, with trembling lips and with tears suddenly glistening on his eyelashes, began speaking in an imploring voice.

"Alexey Ivanovitch, save, save me, spare me."

It was a long while before I could understand. He kept talking and talking and talking, continually repeating, "Spare me, spare me!" At last I guessed that he expected something in the way of advice from me; or, rather, abandoned by all in his misery and anxiety, he had thought of me and had sent for me, simply to talk and talk and talk to me.

He was mad, or at any rate utterly distraught. He clasped his hands and was on the point of dropping on his knees before me to implore me (what do you suppose?) to go at once to Mlle. Blanche and to beseech, to urge her to return to him and marry him.

"Upon my word, General," I cried; "why, Mlle. Blanche is perhaps scarcely aware of my existence. What can I do?"

But it was vain to protest; he didn't understand what was said to him. He fell to talking about Granny, too, but with terrible incoherence; he was still harping on the idea of sending for the police.

"Among us, among us," he began, suddenly boiling over with indignation; "among us, in a well-ordered state, in fact, where there is a Government in control of things, such old women would have been put under guardianship at once! Yes, my dear sir, yes," he went on, suddenly dropping into a scolding tone, jumping up from his chair and pacing about the room; "you may not be aware of the fact, honoured sir," he said, addressing some imaginary "honoured sir" in the corner, "so let me tell you . . . yes . . . among us such old women are kept in order, kept in order; yes, indeed. . . . Oh, damn it all!"

And he flung himself on the sofa again, and a minute later, almost sobbing, gasping for breath, hastened to tell me that Mlle. Blanche would not marry him because Granny had come instead of the telegram, and that now it was clear he would not come into the inheritance. He imagined that I knew nothing of this till then. I began to speak of De Grieux; he waved his hand: "He has gone away! Everything of mine he has in pawn; I'm stripped of everything! That money you brought . . . that money — I don't know how much there is, I think seven hundred francs are left and that's enough, that's all and what's to come — I don't know, I don't know! . . ."

"How will you pay your hotel bill?" I cried in alarm; "and . . . afterwards what will you do?"

He looked at me pensively, but I fancy he did not understand and perhaps did not hear what I said. I tried to speak of Polina Alexandrovna, of the children; he hurriedly answered: "Yes! yes!" but at once fell to talking of the Prince again, saying that Blanche would go away with him now and "then . . . then, what am I to do, Alexey Ivanovitch?" he asked, addressing me suddenly. "I vow, by God! I don't know what to do; tell me, isn't this ingratitude! Isn't this ingratitude?"

Finally he dissolved into floods of tears.

There was no doing anything with such a man; it would be dangerous to leave him alone, too — something might happen to him. I got rid of him somehow, but let nurse know she must look in upon him pretty frequently, and also spoke to the corridor attendant, a very sensible fellow; he, too, promised me to keep an eye on the General.

I had hardly left the General when Potapitch came to summon me to Granny. It was eight o'clock and she had only just come back from the Casino after losing everything. I went to her; the old lady was sitting in an armchair, utterly worn out and evidently ill. Marfa was giving her a cup of tea and almost forcing her to drink it. And Granny's tone and voice were utterly changed.

"Good-day, Alexey Ivanovitch, my good sir," she said, bending her head slowly, and with dignity; "excuse me for troubling you once more, you must excuse an old woman. I have left everything behind there, my friend, nearly a hundred thousand roubles. You did well not to come with me yesterday. Now I have no money, not a farthing. I don't want to delay a moment, at half-past nine I'm setting off. I have sent to that Englishman of yours — what's his name, Astley — I want to ask him to lend me three thousand francs for a week. So you must persuade him not to take it amiss and refuse. I am still fairly well off, my friend. I have still three villages and two houses. And there is still some money. I didn't bring it all with me. I tell you this that he may not feel any doubts . . . Ah, here he is! One can see he is a nice man."

Mr. Astley had hastened to come at Granny's first summons. With no hesitation and without wasting words he promptly counted out three thousand francs for an I O U which Granny signed. When this business was settled he made haste to take his leave and go away.

"And now you can go, too, Alexey Ivanovitch. I have only a little over an hour left. I want to lie down: my bones ache. Don't be hard on an old fool like me. Henceforward I won't blame young people for being flighty, and it would be a sin for me now to blame that luckless fellow, your General, either. I won't give him any money, though, as he wants me to, because — to my thinking he is utterly silly; only, old fool as I am, I've no more sense than he. Verily God seeks out and punishes pride, even in old age. Well, good-bye. Marfa, lift me up!"

I wanted to see Granny off, however. What's more, I was in a state of suspense; I kept expecting that in another minute something would happen. I could not sit quietly in my room. I went out into the corridor, even for a moment went for a saunter along the avenue. My letter to her had been clear and decisive and the present catastrophe was, of course, a final one. I heard in the hotel that De Grieux had left. If she rejected me as a friend, perhaps she would not reject me as a servant. I was necessary to her, I was of use to her, if only to run her errands, it was bound to be so!

When the train was due to start I ran to the station and saw Granny into the train. Her whole party were together, in a special reserved compartment. "Thank you, my good friend, for your disinterested sympathy," she said, at parting from me; "and tell Praskovya, in reference to what we were discussing yesterday, I shall expect her."

I went home. Passing the General's rooms I met the old nurse and inquired after the General. "Oh, he's all right, sir," she answered me dolefully. I went in, however, but stood still in positive amazement. Mlle. Blanche and the General were both laughing heartily. Madame de Cominges was sitting on the sofa close by. The General was evidently beside himself with delight. He was murmuring incoherently and going off into prolonged fits of nervous laughter, during which his face was puckered with innumerable wrinkles and his eyes disappeared from sight. Afterwards I learnt from Blanche herself that, having dismissed the Prince and having heard how the General was weeping, she had taken it into her head to comfort him by going to see him for a minute. But the poor General did not know that at that time his fate was decided, and that Mlle. Blanche had already packed to set off for Paris by the first train next morning.

Stopping in the doorway of the General's study, I changed my mind and went away unnoticed. Going up to my own room and opening the door, I suddenly noticed a figure in the half-darkness sitting on a chair in the corner by the window. She did not get up when I went in. I went up quickly, looked, and — my heart stood still: it was Polina.

CHAPTER XIV

I POSITIVELY CRIED out aloud.

"What is it? What is it?" she asked me strangely. She was pale and looked gloomy.

"You ask what is it? You? Here in my room!"

"If I come, then I come *altogether*. That's my way. You'll see that directly; light the candle."

I lighted a candle. She got up, went up to the table, and put before me an open letter.

"Read it," she ordered me.

"It's — it's De Grieux's handwriting," I cried, taking the letter. My hands trembled and the lines danced before my eyes. I have forgotten the exact wording of the letter, but here is the main drift of it, if not the actual words.

"Mademoiselle," wrote De Grieux, "an unfortunate circumstance compels me to go away at once. You have, no doubt, observed that I have purposely avoided a final explanation with you until such time as the whole position might be cleared up. The arrival of your old relation (*de la vielle dame*) and her absurd behaviour have put an end to my doubts. The unsettled state of my own affairs forbids me from cherishing further the sweet hopes which I permitted myself to indulge for some time. I regret the past, but I trust that you will not detect in my behaviour anything unworthy of a gentleman and an honest man (*gentilhomme et honnête homme*). Having lost almost all my money in loans to your stepfather, I find myself compelled to make the utmost use of what is left to me; I have already sent word to my friend in Petersburg to arrange at once for the sale of the estates he has mortgaged to me; knowing, however, that your frivolous stepfather has squandered your private fortune I have determined to forgive him fifty thousand francs, and I am returning him part of my claims on his property equivalent to that sum, so that you are now put in a position to regain all that you have lost by demanding the property from him by legal process. I hope, Mademoiselle, that in the present position of affairs my action will be very advantageous to you. I hope, too, that by this action I am fully performing the duty of a man and a gentleman. Rest assured that your memory is imprinted upon my heart for ever."

"Well, that's all clear," I said, turning to Polina; "surely you could have expected nothing else," I added, with indignation.

"I expected nothing," she answered, with apparent composure, though there was a tremor in her voice; "I had made up my mind long ago; I read his mind and knew what he was thinking. He thought that I was trying — that I should insist . . ." (She broke off without finishing her sentence, bit her lips and was silent.) "I purposely doubled my scorn towards him," she began again. "I waited to see what was coming from him. If a telegram had come telling of the inheritance I'd have flung him the money borrowed from that idiot, my stepfather, and would have sent him about his business. He has been hateful to me for ages and ages. Oh! he was not the same man! a thousand times over, I tell you, he was different! but now, now . . . Oh, with what happiness I could fling that fifty thousand in his nasty face and spit and stamp . . ."

"But the security, the I O U for that fifty thousand, is in the General's hands. Take it and return it to De Grieux."

"Oh, that's not the same thing, that's not the same thing . . ."

"Yes, that's true, it's not the same thing. Besides, what is the General capable of now? And Granny!" I cried suddenly.

Polina looked at me, as it were absent-mindedly and impatiently.

"Why Granny?" asked Polina, with vexation. "I can't go to her . . . And I don't want to ask any one's pardon," she added irritably.

"What's to be done!" I cried, "and how, oh, how could you love De Grieux! Oh, the scoundrel, the scoundrel! If you like I will kill him in a duel! Where is he now?"

"He's at Frankfurt, and will be there three days."

"One word from you and I'll set off to-morrow by the first train," I said, with stupid enthusiasm.

She laughed.

"Why, he'll say, maybe: 'Give me back the fifty thousand francs first.' Besides, what should you fight him for? . . . What nonsense it is!"

"But where, where is one to get that fifty thousand francs?" I repeated, grinding my teeth as though it had been possible to pick them up from the floor. "I say — Mr. Astley," I suggested, turning to her with a strange idea dawning upon me.

Her eyes flashed.

"What, do you mean to say *you yourself* want me to turn from you to that Englishman!" she said, looking in my face with a searching glance and smiling bitterly. For the first time in her life she addressed me in the second person singular.

I believe she was giddy with emotion at the moment, and all at once she sat down on the sofa as though she were exhausted.

It was as though I had been struck by a flash of lightning. I stood up and could not believe my eyes, could not believe my ears! Why, then she loved me! She had come to me and not to Mr. Astley!

She, she, a young girl, had come to my room in an hotel, so she had utterly compromised herself by her own act, and I, I was standing before her and still did not understand.

One wild idea flashed through my mind.

"Polina, give me only one hour. Stay here only one hour and . . . I'll come back. That's . . . that's essential! You shall see! Be here, be here!"

And I ran out of the room, not responding to her amazed and questioning look; she called something after me but I did not turn back.

Sometimes the wildest idea, the most apparently impossible thought, takes possession of one's mind so strongly that one accepts it at last as something substantial . . . more than that, if the idea is associated with a strong passionate desire, then sometimes one will accept it at last as something fated, inevitable, predestined — as something bound to be, and bound to happen. Perhaps there is something else in it, some combination of presentiments, some extraordinary effort of will, self-poisoning by one's own fancy — or something else — I don't know what, but on that evening (which I shall never in my life forget) something marvellous happened to me. Though it is quite justified by the laws of arithmetic, nevertheless it is a marvel to me to this day. And why, why had that conviction so long before taken such firm and deep root in my mind? I had certainly thought about it — I repeat — not as a chance among others which might or might not come to pass, but as something which was absolutely bound to happen!

It was a quarter past ten. I went into the Casino with a confident expectation and at the same time with an excitement I had never experienced before. There were still a good many people in the gambling hall, though not half as many as in the morning.

Between ten and eleven there are still to be found in the gambling halls the genuine desperate gamblers for whom nothing exists at a spa but roulette, who have come for that alone, who scarcely notice what is going on around them and take no interest in anything during the whole season, but play from morning till night and would be ready perhaps to play all night till dawn, too, if it were possible. And they always disperse with annoyance when at twelve o'clock the roulette hall is closed. And when the senior croupier announces, just before midnight, "*Les trois derniers coups, messieurs*," they are ready to stake on those last three strokes all they have in their pockets — and do, in fact, lose most at that time. I went up to the very table where Granny had sat that day. It was not crowded, and so I soon took my place at the table standing. Exactly before me was the word "Passe" scrawled on the green cloth.

"Passe" is the series of numbers from nineteen inclusive to thirty-six. The first series of numbers from one to eighteen inclusive is called "Manque"; but what was that to me? I was not calculating, I had not even heard what had been the winning number last, and I did not ask about it when I began to play — as every player of any prudence would do. I pulled out all my twenty friedrichs d'or and staked them on "passe," the word which lay before me.

"Vingt deux," cried the croupier.

I had won and again staked all: including my winnings.

"Trente et un," cried the croupier.

I had won again. I had in all eighty friedrichs d'or. I staked the whole of that sum on the twelve middle numbers (my winnings would be three to one, but the chances were two to one against me). The wheel rotated and stopped at twenty-four. I was passed three rolls each of fifty friedrichs d'or in paper and ten gold coins; I had now two hundred friedrichs d'or.

I was as though in delirium and I moved the whole heap of gold to red — and suddenly thought better of it. And for the only time that whole evening, all the time I was playing, I felt chilled with terror and a shudder made my arms and legs tremble, I felt with horror and instantly realized what losing would mean for me now! My whole life was at stake.

"Rouge," cried the croupier, and I drew a breath; fiery pins and needles were tingling all over my body. I was paid in banknotes. It came to four thousand florins and eighty friedrichs d'or (I could still keep count at that stage).

Then, I remember, I staked two thousand florins on the twelve middle numbers, and lost: I staked my gold, the eighty friedrichs d'or, and lost. I was seized with fury: I snatched up the two hundred florins I had left and staked them on the first twelve numbers — haphazard, at random, without thinking! There was, however, an instant of suspense, like, perhaps, the feeling experienced by Madame Blanchard when she flew from a balloon in Paris to the earth.

"Quatre!" cried the croupier.

Now with my stake I had six thousand florins. I looked triumphant already. I was afraid of nothing—nothing, and staked four thousand florins on black. Nine people followed my example and staked on black. The croupiers exchanged glances and said something to one another. People were talking all round in suspense.

Black won. I don't remember my winnings after, nor what I staked on. I only remember as though in a dream that I won, I believe, sixteen thousand florins; suddenly three unlucky turns took twelve thousand from it; then I staked the last four thousand on "passe" (but I scarcely felt anything as I did so; I simply waited in a mechanical, senseless way)— and again I won; then I won four times running. I only remember that I gathered up money in thousands; I remember, too, that the middle twelve won most often and I kept to it. It turned up with a sort of regularity, certainly three or four times in succession, then it did not turn up twice running and then it followed three or four times in succession. Such astonishing regularity is sometimes met with in streaks, and that is what throws inveterate gamblers who calculate with a pencil in their hands out of their reckoning. And what horrible ironies of fate happen sometimes in such cases!

I believe not more than half an hour had passed since I came into the room, when suddenly the croupier informed me that I had won thirty thousand florins, and as the bank did not meet claims for a larger sum at one time the roulette would be closed till next morning. I snatched up all my gold, dropped it into my pockets, snatched up all my notes, and at once went into the other room where there was another roulette table; the whole crowd streamed after me; there at once a place was cleared for me and I fell to staking again haphazard without reckoning. I don't understand what saved me!

At times, however, a glimmer of prudence began to dawn upon my mind. I clung to certain numbers and combinations, but soon abandoned them and staked almost unconsciously. I must have been very absent-minded; I remember the croupiers several times corrected me. I made several gross mistakes. My temples were soaked with sweat and my hands were shaking. The Poles ran up, too, with offers of their services, but I listened to no one. My luck was unbroken! Suddenly there were sounds of loud talk and laughter, and everyone cried "Bravo, bravo!" some even clapped their hands. Here, too, I collected thirty thousand florins, and the bank closed till next day.

"Go away, go away," a voice whispered on my right.

It was a Frankfurt Jew; he was standing beside me all the time, and I believe sometimes helped me in my play.

"For goodness' sake go," another voice whispered in my left ear.

I took a hurried glance. It was a lady about thirty, very soberly and quietly dressed, with a tired, pale, sickly face which yet bore traces of having once been beautiful. At that moment I was stuffing my pockets with the notes, which I crumpled up anyhow, and gathering up the gold that lay on the table. Snatching up the last roll of notes, I succeeded in putting it into the pale lady's hands quite without attracting notice; I had an intense desire to do so at the time, and I remember her pale slim fingers pressed my hand warmly in token of gratitude. All that took place in one instant.

Having collected quickly all my winnings I went quickly to the trente et quarante.

Trente et quarante is frequented by the aristocratic public. Unlike roulette, it is a game of cards. Here the bank will pay up to a hundred thousand thalers at once. The largest stake is here also four thousand florins. I knew nothing of the game, and scarcely knew how to bet on it, except the red and the black upon which one can bet in this game too. And I stuck to red and black. The whole Casino crowded round. I don't remember whether I once thought of Polina all this time. I was experiencing an overwhelming enjoyment in scooping up and taking away the notes which grew up in a heap before me.

It seemed as though fate were urging me on. This time, as luck would have it, a circumstance occurred which, however, is fairly frequent in the game. Chance favours red, for instance, ten or even fifteen times in succession. I had heard two days before that in the previous week red had turned up twenty-two times in succession; it was something which had never been remembered in roulette, and it was talked of with amazement. Every one, of course, abandoned red at once, and after the tenth time, for instance, scarcely any one dared to stake on it. But none of the experienced players staked on black either. The experienced gambler knows what is meant by this "freak of chance." It would mean that after red had won sixteen times, at the seventeenth time the luck would infallibly fall on black. Novices at play rush to this conclusion in crowds, double and treble their stakes, and lose terribly.

But, noticing that red had turned up seven times running, by strange perversity I staked on it. I am convinced that vanity was half responsible for it; I wanted to impress the spectators by taking a mad risk, and — oh, the strange sensation — I remember distinctly that, quite apart from the promptings of vanity, I was possessed by an intense craving for risk. Perhaps passing through so many sensations my soul was not satisfied but only irritated by them and craved still more sensation — and stronger and stronger ones — till utterly exhausted. And, truly I am not lying, if the regulations had allowed me to stake fifty thousand florins at once, I should certainly have staked them. People around shouted that it was madness — that red had won fourteen times already!

"*Monsieur a gagné déjà cent mille florins,*" I heard a voice say near me.

I suddenly came to myself. What? I had won during that evening a hundred thousand florins! And what more did I want? I fell on my banknotes, crumpled them up in my pockets without counting them, scooped up all my gold, all my rolls of notes, and ran out of the Casino. Every one was laughing as I went through the room, looking at my bulging pockets and at the way I staggered under the weight of gold. I think it weighed over twenty pounds. Several hands were held out to me; I gave it away in handfuls as I snatched it up. Two Jews stopped me at the outer door.

"You are bold — you are very bold," they said to me, "but be sure to go away to-morrow as soon as possible, or else you will lose it all — you will lose it all . . ."

I didn't listen to them. The avenue was so dark that I could not see my hand before my face. It was half a mile to the hotel. I had never been afraid of thieves or robbers even as a small boy; I did not think of them now either. I don't remember what I thought of on the road; I had no thoughts. I was only aware of an immense enjoyment — success, victory, power — I don't know how to express it. Polina's image hovered before my mind too; I remembered her and was conscious I was going to her; I should be with her in a moment, should be telling her and showing her . . . But I hardly remembered what she had said to me earlier, and why I had gone, and all the sensations I had felt, not more than an hour and a half before, seemed to me something long past, transformed, grown old — something of which we should say no more because everything now would begin anew. Almost at the end of the avenue a sudden panic came upon me. What if I were robbed and murdered at this instant? At every step my panic grew greater. I almost ran. Suddenly, at the end of the avenue there was the glare of our hotel with its many windows lighted up — thank God, home!

I ran up to my storey and rapidly opened the door. Polina was there, sitting on the sofa with her arms crossed, with a lighted candle before her. She looked at me with amazement, and no doubt at that moment I must have looked rather strange. I stood before her and began flinging down all my piles of money on the table.

CHAPTER XV

I REMEMBER SHE fixed a very intent look on my face, but without even moving from her seat or changing her position.

"I've won two hundred thousand francs!" I cried, as I flung down the last roll of notes.

The huge bundles of notes and piles of gold filled up the whole table; I could not take my eyes off it. At moments I completely forgot Polina. At one moment I began arranging the heap of banknotes, folding them up together, at the next I began undoing the rolls of gold and heaping them up in one pile; then I abandoned it all and strode rapidly up and down the room, lost in thought, then went up to the table, counting the money again. Suddenly, as though coming to myself, I ran to the door and locked it with two turns of the key. Then I stood pondering before my little portmanteau.

"Shall I put it in the portmanteau till to-morrow?" I said, suddenly remembering Polina and turning towards her.

She was still sitting in the same place without stirring, but watching me attentively. Her expression was somehow strange; I did not like that expression. I am not mistaken if I say that there was hatred in it.

I went up to her quickly.

"Polina, here are twenty-five thousand florins—that's fifty thousand francs—more, in fact. Take it, throw it in his face to-morrow."

She did not answer me.

"If you like I will take you away early in the morning. Shall I?"

She suddenly burst out laughing. She laughed for a long time.

I looked at her with wonder and a mortified feeling. That laugh was very much like sarcastic laughter at my expense, which had always been so frequent at the times of my most passionate declarations.

At last she ceased laughing and frowned; she looked at me sternly from under her brows.

"I won't take your money," she declared contemptuously.

"How? What's this?" I cried. "Polina, why?"

"I won't take money for nothing."

"I offer it you as a friend; I offer you my life."

She looked at me with a long, penetrating look, as though she would pierce me through with it.

"You give too much," she said, with a laugh; "De Grieux's mistress is not worth fifty thousand francs."

"Polina, how can you talk to me like that!" I cried, reproachfully. "Am I a De Grieux?"

"I hate you! Yes . . . yes! . . . I love you no more than De Grieux," she cried, her eyes suddenly flashing.

Then she suddenly covered her face with her hands and went into hysterics. I rushed to her.

I realized that something had happened to her while I was away. She seemed quite out of her mind.

"Buy me! Do you want to? Do you want to? For fifty thousand francs, like De Grieux?" broke from her with convulsive sobs.

I held her in my arms, kissed her hands, her feet, fell on my knees before her.

Her hysterics passed off. She put both hands on my shoulders, and looked at me intently; she seemed trying to read something in my face. She listened to me, but evidently did not hear what I was saying to her. Some doubt and anxiety betrayed itself in her face. I was anxious about her; it seemed to me that her brain was giving way. Then she began softly drawing me to her; a trustful smile began straying over her face; but she suddenly pushed me away, and again fell to scanning me with a darkened look.

Suddenly she fell to embracing me.

"You love me, you love me, don't you?" she said. "Why, you . . . why, you . . . wanted to fight the Baron for my sake!"

And suddenly she burst out laughing — as though she had recalled something sweet and funny. She cried and laughed all at once. Well, what was I to do? I was in a fever myself. I remember she began saying something to me — but I could scarcely understand anything. It was a sort of delirium — a sort of babble — as though she wanted to tell me something as rapidly as possible — a delirium which was interrupted from time to time with the merriest laughter, which at last frightened me. "No, no; you are sweet, sweet," she repeated. "You are my faithful one!" And again she put her hand on my shoulders, again she looked at me and repeated, "You love me . . . love me . . . will love me?" I could not take my eyes off her; I had never seen her before in such a mood of love and tenderness; it is true this, of course, was delirium, but . . . noticing my passionate expression, she suddenly began smiling slyly; apropos of nothing she began suddenly talking of Mr. Astley.

She talked incessantly of Mr. Astley, however, (she talked of him particularly when she had been trying to tell me of something that evening,) but what she meant exactly I could not quite grasp; she seemed to be actually laughing at him. She repeated continually that he was waiting and that, did I know, he was certainly standing under the window?

"Yes, yes, under the window; come open it: look out: look out: he certainly is here!" She pushed me to the window, but as soon as I made a movement to go she went off into peals of laughter and I remained with her, and she fell to embracing me.

"Shall we go away? shall we go away to-morrow?" The question suddenly came into her mind uneasily. "Well . . ." (and she sank into thought). "Well, shall we overtake Granny; what do you think? I think we might overtake her at Berlin. What do you think she will say when she sees us? And Mr. Astley? . . . Well, he won't leap off the Schlangenberg — what do you think?" (She burst out laughing.) "Come, listen, do you know where he is going next summer? He wants to go to the North Pole for scientific investigations, and he has asked me to go with him, ha-ha-ha! He says that we Russians can do nothing without Europeans and are incapable of anything. . . . But he is good-natured, too! Do you know he makes excuses for the General? He says that Blanche . . . that passion — oh, I don't know, I don't know," she repeated, as though she didn't know what she was talking about. "They are poor — how sorry I am for them, and Granny . . . Come, listen, listen, how could you kill De Grieux? And did you really imagine you could kill him? Oh, silly fellow! Can you really think I would let you fight with De Grieux? Why, you did not even kill the Baron," she added, suddenly laughing. "Oh, how funny you were then with the Baron. I looked at you both from the seat; and how unwilling you were to go then, when I sent you. How I laughed then, how I laughed," she added, laughing.

And suddenly she kissed and embraced me again. Again she pressed her face to mine passionately and tenderly. I heard nothing and thought of nothing more. My head was in a whirl . . .

I think it was about seven o'clock in the morning when I woke up. The sun was shining into the room. Polina was sitting beside me and looking about her strangely, as though she were waking from some darkness and trying to collect her thoughts. She, too, had only just woken up and was gazing at the table and the money. My head ached and was heavy. I tried to take Polina by the hand: she pushed me away and jumped up from the sofa. The dawning day was overcast. Rain had fallen before sunrise. She went to the window, she opened it, put out her head and shoulders and with her face in her hands and her elbows on the window-sill, stayed for three minutes looking out without turning to me or hearing what I said to her. I wondered with dread what would happen now and how it would end. All at once she got up from the window, went up to the table and, looking at me with infinite hatred, with lips trembling with anger, she said to me —

"Well, give me my fifty thousand francs now?"

"Polina, again, again?" I was beginning.

"Or have you changed your mind? Ha-ha-ha! Perhaps you regret it now."

Twenty-five thousand florins, counted out the evening before, were lying on the table; I took the money and gave it to her.

"It's mine now, isn't it? That's so, isn't it? Isn't it?" she asked me, spitefully holding the money in her hand.

"Yes, it was always yours," I answered.

"Well, there are your fifty thousand francs for you!"

With a swing of her arm she flung the money at me. It hit me a stinging blow in the face and the coins flew all over the table. After doing this Polina ran out of the room.

I know that at that moment she was certainly not in her right mind, though I don't understand such temporary insanity. It is true that she is still ill, even now, a month later. What was the cause of her condition, and, above all, of this whim? Was it wounded pride? Despair at having brought herself to come to me? Had I shown any sign of priding myself on my happiness, and did I, like De Grieux, want to get rid of her by giving her fifty thousand francs? But that was not so; I know that, on my conscience. I believe that her vanity was partly responsible; her vanity prompted her to distrust and insult me, although all that perhaps, was not clear, even to herself. In that case, of course, I was punished for De Grieux and was made responsible, though I was not much to blame. It is true that all this was almost only delirium; it is true, too, that I knew she was in delirium and . . . did not take that fact into consideration; perhaps she cannot forgive me for that now. Yes, but that is now; but then, then? Why, she was not in such a delirium and so ill then as to be utterly oblivious of what she was doing; when she came to me with De Grieux's letter she knew what she was doing.

I made haste to thrust all my notes and my heap of gold into the bed, covered it over and went out ten minutes after Polina. I made sure she would run home, and I thought I would slip in to them on the sly, and in the hall ask the nurse how the young lady was. What was my astonishment when I learnt from nurse, whom I met on the stairs, that Polina had not yet returned home and that nurse was coming to me for her.

"She only just left my room about ten minutes ago; where can she have gone?"

Nurse looked at me reproachfully.

And meanwhile it had caused a regular scandal, which by now was all over the hotel. In the porter's room and at the *ober-kellner's* it was whispered that Fraülein had run out of the hotel in the rain at six o'clock in the morning in the direction of the Hôtel d'Angleterre. From what they said and hinted, I noticed that they all knew already that she had spent the night in my room. However, stories were being told of the whole family: it had become known all through the hotel that the General had gone out of his mind and was crying. The story was that Granny was his mother, who had come expressly from Russia to prevent her son's marriage with Mlle. de Cominges, and was going to cut him out of her will if he disobeyed her, and, as he certainly would disobey her, the Countess had purposely thrown away all her money at roulette before his eyes, so that he should get nothing. "*Diese Russen!*" repeated the *ober-kellner*, shaking his head indignantly. The others laughed. The *ober-kellner* was making out his bill. My winning was known about already. Karl, my corridor attendant, was the first to congratulate me. But I had no thought for any of them. I rushed to the Hôtel d'Angleterre.

It was early; Mr. Astley was seeing no one; learning that it was I, he came out into the corridor to me and stopped before me, turning his pewtery eyes upon me in silence, waiting to hear what I should say. I inquired about Polina.

"She is ill," answered Mr. Astley, looking at me as fixedly as before.

"Then she really is with you?"

"Yes, she is."

"Then, what do you . . . do you mean to keep her?"

"Yes."

"Mr. Astley, it will make a scandal; it's impossible. Besides, she is quite ill; perhaps you don't see it?"

"Oh, yes, I notice it, and I've just told you she is ill. If she had not been ill she would not have spent the night with you."

"Then you know that?"

"Yes, I know it. She came here yesterday and I would have taken her to a relation of mine, but as she was ill, she made a mistake and went to you."

"Fancy that! Well, I congratulate you, Mr. Astley. By the way, you've given me an idea: weren't you standing all night under our window? Miss Polina was making me open the window and look out all night to see whether you were standing under the window; she kept laughing about it."

"Really? No, I didn't stand under the window; but I was waiting in the corridor and walking round."

"But she must be looked after, Mr. Astley."

"Oh, yes, I've sent for the doctor, and, if she dies, you will answer to me for her death."

I was amazed.

"Upon my word, Mr. Astley, what do you want?"

"And is it true that you won two hundred thousand thalers yesterday?"

"Only a hundred thousand florins."

"Well, do you see, you had better go off to Paris this morning!"

"What for?"

"All Russians who have money go to Paris," Mr. Astley explained, in a tone of voice as though he had read this in a book.

"What could I do now in Paris, in the summer? I love her, Mr. Astley, you know it yourself."

"Really? I am convinced you don't. If you remain here you will certainly lose all you have won and you will have nothing left to go to Paris with. But, good-bye, I am perfectly certain you will go to Paris to-day."

"Very well, good-bye, only I shan't go to Paris. Think, Mr. Astley, what will be happening here? The General . . . and now this adventure with Miss Polina — why, that will be all over the town."

"Yes, all over the town; I believe the General is not thinking about that: he has no thoughts to spare for that. Besides, Miss Polina has a perfect right to live where she likes. In regard to that family, one may say quite correctly that the family no longer exists."

I walked away laughing at this Englishman's strange conviction that I was going to Paris. "He wants to shoot me in a duel, though," I thought, "if Mlle. Polina dies — what a complication!" I swear I was sorry for Polina, but, strange to say, from the very moment when I reached the gambling tables the previous evening and began winning a pile of money, my love had retreated, so to speak, into the background. I say this now; but at the time I did not realize all this clearly. Can I really be a gambler? Can I really . . . have loved Polina so strangely? No, I love her to this day. God is my witness! And then, when I left Mr. Astley and went home, I was genuinely miserable and blaming myself. But . . . at this point a very strange and silly thing happened to me.

I was hurrying to see the General, when suddenly, not far from his rooms, a door was opened and some one called me. It was Madame la veuve Cominges, and she called me at the bidding of Mlle. Blanche. I went in to see Mlle. Blanche.

They had a small suite of apartments, consisting of two rooms. I could hear Mlle. Blanche laugh and call out from the bedroom.

She was getting up.

"Ah, c'est lui! Viens donc, bête! Is it true, que tu as gagné une montagne d'or et d'argent? J'aimerais mieux l'or."

"Yes, I did win," I answered, laughing.

"How much?"

"A hundred thousand florins."

"*Bibi, comme tu es bête*. Why, come in here. I can't hear anything. *Nous ferons bombance, n'est-ce pas?*"

I went in to her. She was lying under a pink satin quilt, above which her robust, swarthy, wonderfully swarthy, shoulders were visible, shoulders such as one only sees in one's dreams, covered to some extent by a batiste nightgown bordered with white lace which was wonderfully becoming to her dark skin.

"*Mon fils, as-tu du cœur?*" she cried, seeing me, and burst out laughing. She laughed very good-humouredly, and sometimes quite genuinely.

"*Tout autre*," I began, paraphrasing Corneille.

"Here you see, *vois-tu*," she began babbling; "to begin with, find my stockings, help me to put them on; and then, *si tu n'es pas trop bête, je te prends à Paris*. You know I am just going."

"Just going?"

"In half an hour."

All her things were indeed packed. All her portmanteaus and things were ready. Coffee had been served some time before.

"*Eh bien*, if you like, *tu verras Paris. Dis donc qu'est-ce que c'est qu'un outchitel? Tu étais bien bête, quand tu étais outchitel*. Where are my stockings? Put them on for me?"

She thrust out some positively fascinating feet, little dark-skinned feet, not in the least misshapen, as feet that look so small in shoes always are. I laughed and began drawing her silk stockings on for her. Meanwhile Mlle. Blanche sat up in bed, prattling away.

"*Eh bien, que feras-tu, si je te prends avec?* To begin with, I want fifty thousand francs. You'll give them to me at Frankfurt. *Nous allons à Paris*: there we'll play together: *et je te ferai voir des étoiles en plein jour*. You will see women such as you have never seen before. Listen . . ."

"Wait a minute, so if I give you fifty thousand francs, what will be left for me?"

"*Et cent cinquante mille francs*, you have forgotten: and what's more, I consent to live with you a month, two months: *que sais-je!* In those two months we shall certainly get through that hundred and fifty thousand francs, you see, *je suis bonne enfant*, and I tell you beforehand, *mais tu verras des étoiles*."

"What! all in two months!"

"Why! does that horrify you? *Ah, vil esclave!* But, do you know? one month of such a life is worth your whole existence. One month — *et après le déluge! Mais tu ne peux comprendre; va!* Go along, go along, you are not worth it! *Aie, que fais-tu?*"

At that moment I was putting a stocking on the other leg, but could not resist kissing it. She pulled it away and began hitting me on the head with the tip of her foot. At last, she turned me out altogether.

"*Et bien! mon outchitel, je t'attends, si tu veux*; I am starting in a quarter of an hour!" she called after me.

On returning home I felt as though my head were going round. Well, it was not my fault that Mlle. Polina had thrown the whole pile of money in my face, and had even yesterday preferred Mr. Astley to me. Some of the banknotes that had been scattered about were still lying on the floor; I picked them up. At that moment the door opened and the *ober-kellner* himself made his appearance (he had never deigned to look into my room before) with a suggestion that I might like to move downstairs to a magnificent suite of apartments which had just been vacated by Count V.

I stood still and thought a little.

"My bill — I am just leaving, in ten minutes," I cried. "If it's to be Paris, let it be Paris," I thought to myself; "it seems it was fated at my birth!"

A quarter of an hour later we were actually sitting in a reserved compartment, Mlle. Blanche, Madame la veuve Cominges and I. Mlle. Blanche, looking at me, laughed till she was almost hysterical. Madame de Cominges followed suit; I cannot say that I felt cheerful. My life had broken in two, but since the previous day I had grown used to staking everything on a card. Perhaps it is really the truth that my sudden wealth was too much for me and had turned my head. *Peut-être, je ne demandais pas mieux*. It seemed to me for a time — but only for a time, the scenes were shifted. "But in a month I shall be here, and then . . . and then we will try our strength, Mr. Astley!" No, as I recall it now, I was awfully sad then, though I did laugh as loudly as that idiot, Blanche.

"But what is the matter with you? How silly you are! Oh! how silly you are!" Blanche kept exclaiming, interrupting her laughter to scold me in earnest. "Oh well, oh well, we'll spend your two hundred thousand francs: but in exchange *mais tu seras heureux comme un petit roi*; I will tie your cravat myself and introduce you to Hortense. And when we have spent all our money, you will come back here and break the bank again. What did the Jews tell you? The great thing is — boldness, and you have it, and you will bring me money to Paris more than once again. *Quant à moi je veux cinquante mille francs de rentes et alors . . .*"

"And the General?" I asked her.

"Why, the General, as you know, comes to see me every day with a bouquet. This time I purposely asked him to get me some very rare flowers. The poor fellow will come back and will find the bird has flown. He'll fly after us, you will see. Ha-ha-ha! I shall be awfully pleased to see him. He'll be of use to me in Paris; Mr. Astley will pay his bill here. . . ."

And so that was the way in which I went to Paris.

CHAPTER XVI

WHAT SHALL I say about Paris? It was madness, of course, and foolery. I only spent a little over three weeks in Paris, and by the end of that time my hundred thousand francs was finished. I speak only of a hundred thousand. The other hundred thousand I gave to Mlle. Blanche in hard cash — fifty thousand at Frankfurt and three days later in Paris I gave her an I O U for another fifty thousand francs, though a week later she exchanged this for cash from me. *"Et les cent mille francs, qui nous restent, tu les mangeras avec moi, mon outchitel."* She always called me an *outchitel*, i. e. a tutor. It is difficult to imagine anything in the world meaner, stingier and more niggardly than the class of creatures to which Mlle. Blanche belonged. But that was in the spending of her own money. As regards my hundred thousand francs, she openly informed me, later on, that she needed them to establish herself in Paris, "as now I am going to settle in decent style once for all, and now no one shall turn me aside for a long time; at least, that is my plan," she added. I hardly saw that hundred thousand, however; she kept the money the whole time, and in my purse, into which she looked every day, there was never more than a hundred francs, and always less and less.

"What do you want money for?" she would say, sometimes, in the simplest way, and I did not dispute with her. But she furnished and decorated her flat very nicely with that money, and afterwards, when she took me to her new abode, as she showed me the rooms, she said: "You see what care and taste can do even with the scantiest means." These "scanty means" amounted to fifty thousand francs, however. With the second fifty thousand she provided herself with a carriage and horses. Moreover, we gave two balls, that is, two evening parties at which were present Hortense, Lizette and Cléopatra, women remarkable in very many respects and even quite good-looking. At those two evenings I had to play the very foolish part of host, to receive and entertain the stupidest rich tradesmen, incredibly ignorant and shameless, various army lieutenants and miserable little authors and journalistic insects, who appeared in the most fashionable swallow-tails and straw-coloured gloves, and displayed a vanity and affectation whose proportions were beyond anything conceivable in Petersburg — and that is saying a great deal. Many of them thought fit to jeer at me; but I got drunk with champagne and lolled at full length in a back room. To me it was all loathsome to the last degree. *"C'est un outchitel,"* Blanche kept saying about me, *"il a gagné deux cent mille francs.* Without me he wouldn't have known how to spend it. And afterwards he will be an *outchitel* again; don't you know of a place for one? we ought to do something for him."

I had recourse to champagne very often, because I was often sad and dreadfully bored. I lived in the most bourgeois, in the most mercenary surroundings in which every *sou* was reckoned and accounted for. Blanche disliked me for the first fortnight: I noticed that; it is true, she dressed me like a dandy, and tied my cravat for me every day, but in her soul she genuinely despised me. I did not pay the slightest attention to that. Bored and dispirited, I used to go usually to the Château de Fleurs, where regularly every evening I got drunk and practised the *cancan* (which they dance so disgustingly there), and acquired in the end a kind of celebrity.

At last Blanche gauged my true character. She had for some reason conceived the idea that I should spend all the time we were together walking after her with a pencil and paper in my hand, and should always be reckoning how much she had spent, how much she had stolen, how much she would spend and how much more she would steal. And she was, of course, convinced that we should have a regular battle over every ten-franc piece. She had an answer in readiness for every attack that she anticipated from me; but when she found I did not attack her, she could not at first refrain from defending herself, unprovoked. Sometimes she would begin with great heat, but seeing that I remained silent as a rule, lying on a sofa gazing at the ceiling — at last, she was surprised. At first she thought I was simply stupid, "*un outchitel*," and merely cut short her explanations, probably thinking to herself: "Why, he's a fool. There's no need to lay it on for him, since he doesn't understand." She would go away but come back again ten minutes later (this happened at a time when she was spending most ferociously, spending on a scale quite out of proportion to our means: she had, for instance, got rid of the horses first bought and bought another pair for sixteen thousand francs).

"Well, so you are not cross, bibi?" she said, coming up to me.

"N — n — n — no! You weary me!" I said, removing her hands from me, but this seemed to her so curious, that she immediately sat down beside me.

"You see, I only decided to pay so much because they could be sold later on if need be. They can be sold again for twenty thousand francs."

"No doubt, no doubt; they are splendid horses, and you have a fine turnout now; it suits you; well, that's enough."

"Then you are not cross."

"Why should I be? You are sensible to provide yourself with things that are necessary to you. All that will be of use to you afterwards. I see that it is quite necessary for you to establish yourself in such a style;

otherwise you will never save up your million. Our hundred thousand francs is only a beginning; a drop in the ocean."

Blanche had expected from me anything but such reflections (instead of outcries and reproaches). She seemed to drop from the clouds.

"So that's what you are like! *Mais tu as l'esprit pour comprendre. Sais-tu, mon garçon*, though you are an *outchitel* you ought to have been born a prince. So you don't grudge the money's going so quickly?"

"Bother the money! the quicker the better!"

"*Mais sais-tu . . . mais dis donc*, are you rich? *Mais sais-tu*, you really despise money too much. *Qu'est-ce que tu feras après, dis donc?*"

"*Après*, I shall go to Homburg and win another hundred thousand francs."

"*Oui, oui, c'est ça, c'est magnifique!* And I know you will certainly win it and bring it here. *Dis donc*, why you will make me really love you. *Eh bien*, I will love you all the time for being like that, and won't once be unfaithful to you. You see, I have not loved you all this time, *parce que je croyais que tu n'étais qu'un outchitel (quelque chose comme un laquais, n'est-ce pas?)*, but I have been faithful to you all the same, *parce que je suis bonne fille.*"

"Come, you are lying! How about Albert, that swarthy-faced little officer; do you suppose I didn't see last time?"

"*Oh, oh, mais tu es . . .*"

"Come, you are lying, you are lying; why, do you suppose I should be angry? Why, it's no matter; *il faut que la jeunesse se passe*. And there's no need for you to send him away if you had him before me and are fond of him. Only don't give him money, do you hear?"

"So you are not angry about it? *Mais tu es un vrai philosophe, sais-tu? Un vrai philosophe!*" she cried enthusiastically.

"*Eh bien! je t'aimerai, je t'aimerai — tu verras, tu seras content!*"

And from that time she really did seem to be attached to me, to be really affectionate; and so our last ten days passed. The "stars" promised me I did not see. But in some respects she really did keep her word. What is more, she introduced me to Hortense, who really was a remarkable woman in her own way, and in our circle was called *Thérèse philosophe . . .*

However, there is no need to enlarge upon that; all that might make a separate story, in a different tone, which I do not want to introduce into this story. The fact is, I longed above everything for all this episode to be over. But our hundred thousand francs lasted, as I have mentioned already, almost a month — at which I was genuinely surprised; eighty thousand of that, at least, Blanche spent on things for herself, and we lived on no more than twenty thousand francs, and — yet it was enough.

Blanche, who was in the end almost open with me (or, at any rate, did not lie to me about some things), declared that, anyway, the debts she had been obliged to make would not fall upon me: "I have never given you bills or I O U's to sign," she said, "because I was sorry for you; but any other girl would have certainly done it and got you into prison. You see, you see how I loved you and how good I am! Think of what that devil of a wedding alone is going to cost me!"

We really were going to have a wedding. It took place at the very end of my month, and it may be assumed that the last remains of my hundred thousand francs went upon it; that was how the thing ended; that is, my month ended with that, and after it I received my formal dismissal.

This was how it happened: a week after our arrival in Paris the General suddenly turned up. He came straight to Blanche, and from his first call almost lived with us. He had a lodging of his own, it is true. Blanche received him joyfully, with shrieks of laughter, and even flew to embrace him; as things had turned out, she was unwilling to let him go: and he had to follow her about everywhere, on the boulevards, and to the theatres, and to call on her acquaintances, and to take her for drives. The General was still of use for such purposes; he was of rather imposing and decorous appearance — he was above the average in height, with dyed whiskers and moustaches (he had once served in the Cuirassiers); he was still presentable-looking, though his face was puffy. His manners were superb; he looked well in evening dress. In Paris he began wearing his decorations. The promenade on the boulevard with a man like this was not only possible, but *advantageous*. The good-natured and sense-less General was immensely delighted with all this; he had not reckoned upon it at all when he came to see us on arriving in Paris. He had come, then, almost trembling with terror; he was afraid that Blanche would make an uproar and order him to be turned out; and so he was highly delighted at the changed aspect of the position, and spent the whole month in a sort of senseless rapture: and he was in the same state when I left him. I learnt that on the morning of our sudden departure from Roulettenburg he had had some sort of a fit. He had fallen insensible, and had been all that week almost like a madman, talking incessantly. He was being nursed and doctored, but he suddenly threw up every-thing, got into the train and flew off to Paris. Of course, Blanche's reception was the best cure for him; but the traces of his illness re-mained long after, in spite of his joy and his enthusiastic condition. He was utterly incapable of reflection or even of carrying on a conversation on any serious subject; when any such topic was brought forward, he confined himself to nodding his head and ejaculating, "H'm!" at every word. He often laughed, but it was a nervous, sickly laugh, as though he were giggling; another time he would sit for hours looking as black as night, knitting his bushy brows. Of many things he had no recollection whatever; he had become absent-minded to an unseemly degree, and had acquired the habit of talking to himself. Blanche was the only person who could rouse him; and, indeed, his attacks of gloom and depression, when he hid himself in a corner, meant nothing but that he hadn't seen Blanche for a long time, or that Blanche had gone off somewhere without taking him, or had not been nice to him before going. At the same time he could not say what he wanted, and did not know why he was depressed and miserable. After sitting for two or three hours (I noticed this on two or three occasions when Blanche had gone out for the whole day, probably to see Albert), he would suddenly begin to look about him in a nervous fluster, to stare round, to recollect himself, and seem to be looking for something; but seeing no one and not remembering the question he meant to ask, he sank into forgetfulness again till Blanche reappeared, gay, frisky, gorgeously dressed, with her ringing laugh; she would run up to him, begin teasing him, and even kissing him — a favour which she did not often, however, bestow upon him. Once the General was so delighted to see her that he even burst into tears — I really marvelled at him.

From the very first, Blanche began to plead his cause before me. Indeed, she waxed eloquent on his behalf; reminded me that she had betrayed the General for my sake, that she was almost engaged to him, had given him her word; that he had abandoned his family on her account, and, lastly, that I had been in his service and ought to remember that, and that I ought to be ashamed. . . . I said nothing while she rattled away at a terrific pace. At last I laughed: and with that the matter ended, that is, at first, she thought I was a fool: and at last came to the conclusion that I was a very nice and accommodating man. In fact, I had the good fortune to win in the end the complete approval of that excellent young woman. (Blanche really was, though, a very good-natured girl, — in her own way, of course; I had not such a high opinion of her at first.) "You're a kind and clever man," she used to say to me towards the end, "and . . . and . . . it's only a pity you are such a fool! You never, never, save anything!"

"*Un vrai russe, un calmouk!*" Several times she sent me to take the General for a walk about the streets, exactly as she might send her lapdog out with her footman. I took him, however, to the theatre, and to the Bal-Mabille, and to the restaurants. Blanche gave me the money for this, though the General had some of his own, and he was very fond of taking out his pocket-book before people. But I had almost to use force to prevent him from buying a brooch for seven hundred francs, by which he was fascinated in the Palais Royal and of which he wanted, at all costs, to make Blanche a present. But what was a brooch of seven hundred francs to her? The General hadn't more than a thousand francs altogether. I could never find out where he had got that money from. I imagine it was from Mr. Astley, especially as the latter had paid their bill at the hotel. As for the General's attitude to me all this time, I believe that he did not even guess at my relations with Blanche. Though he had heard vaguely that I had won a fortune, yet he probably supposed that I was with Blanche in the capacity of a private secretary or even a servant. Anyway, he always, as before, spoke to me condescendingly, authoritatively, and even sometimes fell to scolding me. One morning he amused Blanche and me immensely at breakfast. He was not at all ready to take offence, but suddenly he was huffy with me — why? — I don't know to this day. No doubt he did not know himself. In fact, he made a speech without a beginning or an end, *à bâtons-rompus*, shouted that I was an impudent boy, that he would give me a lesson . . . that he would let me know it . . . and so on. But no one could make out anything from it. Blanche went off into peals of laughter. At last he was somehow appeased and taken out for a walk. I noticed sometimes, however, that he grew sad, that he was regretting some one and something, he was missing something, in spite of Blanche's presence. On two such occasions he began talking to me of himself, but could not express himself clearly, alluded to his times in the army, to his deceased wife, to his family affairs, to his property. He would stumble upon some phrase — and was delighted with it and would repeat it a hundred times a day, though perhaps it expressed neither his feelings nor his thoughts. I tried to talk to him about his children: but he turned off the subject with incoherent babbles, and passed hurriedly to another topic: "Yes, yes, my children, you are right, my children!" Only once he grew sentimental — we were with him at the theatre: "Those unhappy children!" he began suddenly. "Yes, sir, those un — happy children!" And several times afterwards that evening he repeated the same words: "unhappy children!" Once, when I began to speak of Polina, he flew into a frenzy. "She's an ungrateful girl," he cried. "She's wicked and ungrateful! She has disgraced her family. If there were laws here I would make her mind her p's and q's. Yes, indeed, yes, indeed!" As for De Grieux, he could not bear even to hear his name: "He has been the ruin of me," he would say, "he has robbed me, he has destroyed me! He has been my nightmare for the last two years! He has haunted my dreams for whole months! It's, it's, it's . . . Oh, never speak to me of him!"

I saw there was an understanding between them, but, as usual, I said nothing. Blanche announced the news to me, first — it was just a week before we parted: "*Il a de la chance*," she babbled. "Granny really is ill this time, and certainly will die. Mr. Astley has sent a telegram. You must admit that the General is her heir, anyway, and even if he were not, he would not interfere with me in anything. In the first place, he has his pension, and in the second place, he will live in a back room and will be perfectly happy. I shall be 'Madame la Générale.' I shall get into a good set" (Blanche was continually dreaming of this), "in the end I shall be a Russian landowner, *j'aurai un château, des moujiks, et puis j'aurai toujours mon million.*"

"Well, what if he begins to be jealous, begins to insist . . . on goodness knows what — do you understand?"

"Oh, no, *non, non, non!* How dare he! I have taken precautions, you needn't be afraid. I have even made him sign some I O U's for Albert. The least thing — and he will be arrested; and he won't dare!"

"Well, marry him . . ."

The marriage was celebrated without any great pomp; it was a quiet family affair. Albert was invited and a few other intimate friends. Hortense, Cléopatra and company were studiously excluded. The bridegroom was extremely interested in his position. Blanche herself tied his cravat with her own hands, and pomaded his head: and in his swallowtailed coat with his white tie he looked *très comme il faut*.

"*Il est pourtant très comme il faut*," Blanche herself observed to me, coming out of the General's room, as though the idea that the General was *très comme il faut* was a surprise even to her. Though I assisted at the whole affair as an idle spectator, yet I took so little interest in the details that I have to a great extent forgotten the course of events. I only remember that Blanche turned out not to be called "de Cominges," and her mamma not to be *la veuve* "Cominges," but "du Placet." Why they had been both "de Cominges" till then, I don't know. But the General remained very much pleased with that, and "du Placet" pleased him, in fact, better than "de Cominges." On the morning of the wedding, fully dressed for the part, he kept walking to and fro in the drawing-room, repeating to himself with a grave and important air, "Mlle. Blanche du Placet! Blanche du Placet, du Placet! . . ." and his countenance beamed with a certain complacency. At church, before the *maire*, and at the wedding breakfast at home, he was not only joyful but proud. There was a change in both of them. Blanche, too, had an air of peculiar dignity.

"I shall have to behave myself quite differently now," she said to me, perfectly seriously: "*mais vois-tu*, I never thought of one very horrid thing: I even fancy, to this day, I can't learn my surname. Zagoryansky, Zagozyansky, Madame la Générale de Sago — Sago, *ces diables de noms russes, enfin madame la générale a quatorze consonnes! Comme c'est agréable, n'est-ce pas?*"

At last we parted, and Blanche, that silly Blanche, positively shed tears when she said good-bye to me. *"Tu étais bon enfant,"* she said, whimpering. *"Je te croyais bête et tu en avais l'air,* but it suits you." And, pressing my hand at parting, she suddenly cried, *"Attends!"* rushed to her boudoir and, two minutes later, brought me a banknote for two thousand francs. That I should never have believed possible! "It may be of use to you. You may be a very learned *outchitel,* but you are an awfully stupid man. I am not going to give you more than two thousand, for you'll lose it gambling, anyway. Well, good-bye! *Nous serons toujours bons amis,* and if you win, be sure to come to me again, *et tu seras heureux!"*

I had five hundred francs left of my own. I had besides a splendid watch that cost a thousand francs, some diamond studs, and so on, so that I could go on a good time longer without anxiety. I am staying in this little town on purpose to collect myself, and, above all, I am waiting for Mr. Astley. I have learnt for a fact that he will pass through the town and stay here for twenty-four hours on business. I shall find out about everything; and then — then I shall go straight to Homburg. I am not going to Roulettenburg; not till next year anyway. They say it is a bad omen to try your luck twice running at the same tables; and Homburg is the real place for play.

CHAPTER XVII

IT IS A year and eight months since I looked at these notes, and only now in sadness and dejection it has occurred to me to read them through. So I stopped then at my going to Homburg. My God! With what a light heart, comparatively speaking, I wrote those last lines! Though not with a light heart exactly, but with a sort of self-confidence, with undaunted hopes! Had I any doubt of myself? And now more than a year and a half has passed, and I am to my own mind, far worse than a beggar! Yes, what is being a beggar? A beggar is nothing! I have simply ruined myself! However, there is nothing I can compare myself with, and there is no need to give myself a moral lecture! Nothing could be stupider than moral reflections at this date! Oh, self-satisfied people, with what proud satisfaction these prattlers prepare to deliver their lectures! If only they knew how thoroughly I understand the loathsomeness of my present position, they would not be able to bring their tongues to reprimand me. Why, what, what can they tell me that I do not know? And is that the point? The point is that — one turn of the wheel, and all will be changed, and those very moralists will be the first (I am convinced of that) to come up to congratulate me with friendly jests. And they will not all turn away from me as they do now. But, hang them all! What am I now? Zero.

What may I be to-morrow? To-morrow I may rise from the dead and begin to live again! There are still the makings of a man in me.

I did, in fact, go to Homburg then, but ... afterwards I went to Roulettenburg again, and to Spa. I have even been in Baden, where I went as valet to the councillor Gintse, a scoundrel, who was my master here. Yes, I was a lackey for five whole months! I got a place immediately after coming out of prison. (I was sent to prison in Roulettenburg for a debt I made here.) Some one, I don't know who, paid my debt — who was it? Was it Mr. Astley? Polina? I don't know, but the debt was paid; two hundred thalers in all, and I was set free. What could I do? I entered the service of this Gintse. He is a young man and frivolous, he liked to be idle, and I could read and write in three languages. At first I went into his service as a sort of secretary at thirty guldens a month; but I ended by becoming a regular valet: he had not the means to keep a secretary; and he lowered my wages; I had nowhere to go, I remained — and in that way became a lackey by my own doing. I had not enough to eat or to drink in his service, but on the other hand, in five months I saved up seventy guldens. One evening in Baden, however, I announced to him that I intended parting from him; the same evening I went to roulette. Oh, how my heart beat! No, it was not money that I wanted. All that I wanted then was that next day all these Gintses, all these *ober-kellners*, all these magnificent Baden ladies — that they might be all talking about me, repeating my story, wondering at me, admiring me, praising me, and doing homage to my new success. All these are childish dreams and desires, but ... who knows, perhaps I should meet Polina again, too, I should tell her, and she would see that I was above all these stupid ups and downs of fate. . . . Oh, it was not money that was dear to me! I knew I should fling it away to some Blanche again and should drive in Paris again for three weeks with a pair of my own horses, costing sixteen thousand francs. I know for certain that I am not mean; I believe that I am not even a spendthrift — and yet with what a tremor, with what a thrill at my heart, I hear the croupier's cry: *trente et un, rouge, impair et passe*, or: *quatre, noir, pair et manque!* With what avidity I look at the gambling table on which louis d'or, friedrichs d'or and thalers lie scattered: on the piles of gold when they are scattered from the croupier's shovel like glowing embers, or at the piles of silver a yard high that lie round the wheel. Even on my way to the gambling hall, as soon as I hear, two rooms away, the clink of the scattered money I almost go into convulsions.

Oh! that evening, when I took my seventy guldens to the gambling table, was remarkable too. I began with ten guldens, staking them again on *passe*. I have a prejudice in favour of *passe*. I lost. I had sixty guldens left in silver money; I thought a little and chose *zéro*. I began staking five guldens at a time on *zéro*; at the third turn the wheel stopped at *zéro*; I almost died of joy when I received one hundred and seventy-five guldens; I had not been so delighted when I won a hundred thousand guldens. I immediately staked a hundred guldens on *rouge* — it won; the two hundred on *rouge* — it won; the whole of the four hundred on *noir* — it won; the whole eight hundred on *manque* — it won; altogether with what I had before it made one thousand seven hundred guldens and that — in less than five minutes! Yes, at moments like that one forgets all one's former failures! Why, I had gained this by risking more than life itself, I dared to risk it, and — there I was again, a man among men.

I took a room at the hotel, locked myself in and sat till three o'clock counting over my money. In the morning I woke up, no longer a lackey. I determined the same day to go to Homburg: I had not been a lackey or been in prison there. Half an hour before my train left, I set off to stake on two hazards, no more, and lost fifteen hundred florins. Yet I went to Homburg all the same, and I have been here for a month. . . .

I am living, of course, in continual anxiety. I play for the tiniest stakes, and I keep waiting for something, calculating, standing for whole days at the gambling table and watching the play; I even dream of playing — but I feel that in all this, I have, as it were, grown stiff and wooden, as though I had sunk into a muddy swamp. I gather this from my feeling when I met Mr. Astley. We had not seen each other since that time, and we met by accident. This was how it happened: I was walking in the gardens and reckoning that now I was almost without money, but that I had fifty guldens — and that I had, moreover, three days before paid all I owed at the hotel. And so it was possible for me to go once more to roulette — if I were to win anything, I might be able to go on playing; if I lost I should have to get a lackey's place again, if I did not come across Russians in want of a tutor. Absorbed in these thoughts, I went my daily walk, across the park and the forest in the adjoining principality.

Sometimes I used to walk like this for four hours at a time, and go back to Homburg hungry and tired. I had scarcely gone out of the gardens into the park, when suddenly I saw on one of the seats Mr. Astley. He saw me before I saw him, and called to me. I sat down beside him. Detecting in him a certain dignity of manner, I instantly moderated my delight; though I was awfully delighted to see him.

"And so you are here! I thought I should meet you," he said to me. "Don't trouble yourself to tell me your story; I know, I know all about it; I know every detail of your life during this last year and eight months."

"Bah! What a watch you keep on your old friends!" I answered. "It is very creditable in you not to forget. . . . Stay, though, you have given me an idea. Wasn't it you bought me out of prison at Roulettenburg where I was imprisoned for debt for two hundred guldens? Some unknown person paid it for me."

"No, oh, no; it was not I who bought you out when you were in prison at Roulettenburg for a debt of two hundred guldens. But I knew that you were imprisoned for a debt of two hundred guldens."

"Then you know who did pay my debt?"

"Oh, no, I can't say that I know who bought you out."

"Strange; I don't know any of our Russians; besides, the Russians here, I imagine, would not do it; at home in Russia the orthodox may buy out other orthodox Christians. I thought it must have been some eccentric Englishman who did it as a freak."

Mr. Astley listened to me with some surprise. I believe he had expected to find me dejected and crushed.

"I am very glad, however, to find that you have quite maintained your independence of spirit and even your cheerfulness," he pronounced, with a rather disagreeable air.

"That is, you are chafing inwardly with vexation at my not being crushed and humiliated," I said, laughing.

He did not at once understand, but when he understood, he smiled.

"I like your observations: I recognize in those words my clever, enthusiastic and, at the same time, cynical old friend; only Russians can combine in themselves so many opposites at the same time. It is true, a man likes to see even his best friend humiliated; a great part of friendship rests on humiliation. But in the present case I assure you, that I am genuinely glad that you are not dejected. Tell me, do you intend to give up gambling?"

"Oh, damn! I shall give it up at once as soon as I . . ."

"As soon as you have won back what you have lost! Just what I thought; you needn't say any more — I know — you have spoken unawares, and so you have spoken the truth. Tell me, have you any occupation except gambling?"

"No, none. . . ."

He began cross-examining me. I knew nothing. I scarcely looked into the newspapers, and had literally not opened a single book all that time.

"You've grown rusty," he observed. "You have not only given up life, all your interests, private and public, the duties of a man and a citizen, your friends (and you really had friends) — you have not only given up your objects, such as they were, all but gambling — you have even given up your memories. I remember you at an intense and ardent moment of your life; but I am sure you have forgotten all the best feelings you had then; your dreams, your most genuine desires now do not rise above *pair, impair, rouge, noir*, the twelve middle numbers, and so on, I am sure!"

"Enough, Mr. Astley, please, please don't remind me," I cried with vexation, almost with anger, "let me tell you, I've forgotten absolutely nothing; but I've only for a time put everything out of my mind, even my memories, until I can make a radical improvement in my circumstances; then . . . then you will see, I shall rise again from the dead!"

"You will be here still in ten years' time," he said. "I bet you I shall remind you of this on this very seat, if I'm alive."

"Well, that's enough," I interrupted impatiently; "and to prove to you that I am not so forgetful of the past, let me ask: where is Miss Polina now? If it was not you who got me out of prison, it must have been her doing. I have had no news of her of any sort since that time."

"No, oh no, I don't believe she did buy you out. She's in Switzerland now, and you'll do me a great favour if you leave off asking about Miss Polina," he said resolutely, and even with some anger.

"That means that she has wounded you very much!" I laughed with displeasure.

"Miss Polina is of all people deserving of respect the very best, but I repeat—you will do me a great favour if you cease questioning me concerning Miss Polina. You never knew her: and her name on your lips I regard as an insult to my moral feelings."

"You don't say so! you are wrong, however; besides, what have I to talk to you about except that, tell me that? Why all our memories really amount to that! Don't be uneasy, though; I don't want to know your private secret affairs. . . . I am only interested, so to say, in Miss Polina's external affairs. That you could tell me in a couple of words."

"Certainly, on condition that with those two words all is over. Miss Polina was ill for a long time; she's ill even now. For some time she stayed with my mother and sister in the north of England. Six months ago, her grandmother—you remember that madwoman?—died and left her, personally, a fortune of seven thousand pounds. At the present time Miss Polina is travelling with the family of my married sister. Her little brother and sister, too, were provided for by their grandmother's will, and are at school in London. The General, her stepfather, died a month ago in Paris of a stroke. Mlle. Blanche treated him well, but succeeded in getting possession of all he received from the grandmother. . . . I believe that's all."

"And De Grieux? Is not he travelling in Switzerland, too?"

"No, De Grieux is not travelling in Switzerland: and I don't know where De Grieux is; besides, once for all, I warn you to avoid such insinuations and ungentlemanly coupling of names, or you will certainly have to answer for it to me."

"What! in spite of our friendly relations in the past?"

"Yes, in spite of our friendly relations in the past."

"I beg a thousand pardons, Mr. Astley. But allow me, though: there is nothing insulting or ungentlemanly about it; I am not blaming Miss Polina for anything. Besides—a Frenchman and a Russian young lady, speaking generally—it's a combination, Mr. Astley, which is beyond your or my explaining or fully comprehending."

"If you will not mention the name of De Grieux in company with another name, I should like you to explain what you mean by the expression of 'the Frenchman and the Russian young lady?' What do you mean by that 'combination?' Why the Frenchman exactly and why the Russian young lady?"

"You see you are interested. But that's a long story, Mr. Astley. You need to understand many things first. But it is an important question, however absurd it may seem at first sight. The Frenchman, Mr. Astley, is the product of a finished beautiful tradition. You, as a Briton, may not agree with this; I, as a Russian, do not either, from envy maybe; but our young ladies may be of a different opinion. You may think Racine artificial, affected and perfumed; probably you won't even read him. I, too, think him artificial, affected and perfumed—from one point of view even absurd; but he is charming, Mr. Astley, and, what is more, he is a great poet, whether we like it or not. The national type of Frenchman, or, rather, of Parisian, had been moulded into elegant forms while we were still bears. The revolution inherited the traditions of the aristocracy. Now even the vulgarest Frenchman has manners, modes of address, expressions and even thoughts, of perfectly elegant form, though his own initiative, his own soul and heart, have had no part in the creation of that form; it has all come to him through inheritance. Well, Mr. Astley, I must inform you now that there is not a creature on the earth more confiding, and more candid than a good, clean and not too sophisticated Russian girl. De Grieux, appearing in a peculiar rôle, masquerading, can conquer her heart with extraordinary ease; he has elegance of form, Mr. Astley, and the young lady takes this form for his individual soul, as the natural form of his soul and his heart, and not as an external garment, which has come to him by inheritance. Though it will greatly displease you, I must tell you that Englishmen are for the most part awkward and inelegant, and Russians are rather quick to detect beauty, and are eager for it. But to detect beauty of soul and originality of character needs incomparably more independence and freedom than is to be found in our women, above all in our young ladies — and of course ever so much more experience. Miss Polina — forgive me, the word is spoken and one can't take it back — needs a long, long time to bring herself to prefer you to the scoundrel De Grieux. She thinks highly of you, becomes your friend, opens all her heart to you; but yet the hateful scoundrel, the base and petty money-grubber, De Grieux, will still dominate her heart. Mere obstinacy and vanity, so to say, will maintain his supremacy, because at one time this De Grieux appeared to her with the halo of an elegant marquis, a disillusioned liberal, who is supposed to have ruined himself to help her family and her frivolous stepfather. All these shams have been discovered later on. But the fact that they have been discovered makes no difference: anyway, what she wants is the original De Grieux — that's what she wants! And the more she hates the present De Grieux the more she pines for the original one, though he existed only in her imagination. You are a sugar-boiler, Mr. Astley."

"Yes, I am a partner in the well-known firm, Lovel & Co."

"Well, you see, Mr. Astley, on one side — a sugar-boiler, and on the other — Apollo Belvedere; it is somewhat incongruous. And I am not even a sugar-boiler; I am simply a paltry gambler at roulette, and have even been a lackey, which I think Miss Polina knows very well, as I fancy she has good detectives."

"You are exasperated, and that is why you talk all this nonsense," Mr. Astley said coolly, after a moment's thought. "Besides, there is nothing original in what you say."

"I admit that! But the awful thing is, my noble friend, that however stale, however hackneyed, however farcical my statements may be — they are nevertheless true! Anyway, you and I have made no way at all!"

"That's disgusting nonsense . . . because, because . . . let me tell you!" Mr. Astley, with flashing eyes, pronounced in a quivering voice, "let me tell you, you ungrateful, unworthy, shallow and unhappy man, that I am come to Homburg expressly at her wish, to see you, to have a long and open conversation with you and to tell her everything — what you are feeling, thinking, hoping, and . . . what you remember!"

"Is it possible! Is it possible?" I cried, and tears rushed in streams from my eyes.

I could not restrain them. I believe it was the first time it happened in my life.

"Yes, unhappy man, she loved you, and I can tell you that, because you are — a lost man! What is more, if I were to tell you that she loves you to this day — you would stay here just the same! Yes, you have destroyed yourself. You had some abilities, a lively disposition, and were not a bad fellow; you might have even been of service to your country, which is in such need of men, but—you will remain here, and your life is over. I don't blame you. To my mind all Russians are like that, or disposed to be like that. If it is not roulette it is something similar. The exceptions are very rare. You are not the first who does not understand the meaning of work (I am not talking of your peasantry). Roulette is a game pre-eminently for the Russians. So far you've been honest and preferred serving as a lackey to stealing. . . . But I dread to think what may come in the future. Enough, good-bye! No doubt you are in want of money? Here are ten louis d'or from me. I won't give you more, for you'll gamble it away in any case. Take it and good-bye! Take it!"

"No, Mr. Astley, after all you have said."

"Ta—ake it!" he cried. "I believe that you are still an honourable man, and I give it as a true friend gives to another friend. If I were sure that you would throw up gambling, leave Homburg and would return to your own country, I would be ready to give you at once a thousand pounds to begin a new career. But I don't give you a thousand pounds: I give you only ten louis d'or just because a thousand pounds and ten louis d'or are just the same to you now; it's all the same—you'll gamble it away. Take it and good-bye."

"I will take it if you will let me embrace you at parting."

"Oh, with pleasure!"

We embraced with sincere feeling, and Mr. Astley went away.

No, he is wrong! If I was crude and silly about Polina and De Grieux, he was crude and hasty about Russians. I say nothing of myself. However . . . however, all that is not the point for the time: that is all words, words, and words, deeds are what are wanted! Switzerland is the great thing now! To-morrow . . . Oh, if only it were possible to set off to-morrow! To begin anew, to rise again. I must show them. . . . Let Polina know that I still can be a man. I have only to . . . But now it's too late—but to-morrow . . . oh, I have a presentiment and it cannot fail to be! I have now fifteen louis d'or, and I have begun with fifteen guldens! If one begins carefully . . . and can I, can I be such a baby! Can I fail to understand that I am a lost man, but—can I not rise again! Yes! I have only for once in my life to be prudent and patient and—that is all! I have only for once to show will power and in one hour I can transform my destiny! The great thing is will power. Only remember what happened to me seven months ago at Roulettenburg just before my final failure. Oh! it was a remarkable instance of determination: I had lost everything then, everything. . . . I was going out of the Casino, I looked, there was still one gulden in my waistcoat pocket: "Then I shall have something for dinner," I thought. But after I had gone a hundred paces I changed my mind and went back. I staked that gulden on *manque* (that time it was on *manque*), and there really is something peculiar in the feeling when, alone in a strange land, far from home and from friends, not knowing whether you will have anything to eat that day — you stake your last last gulden, your very last! I won, and twenty minutes later I went out of the Casino, having a hundred and seventy guldens in my pocket. That's a fact! That's what the last gulden can sometimes do! And what if I had lost heart then? What if I had not dared to risk it? . . .

To-morrow, to-morrow it will all be over!

DOVER·THRIFT·EDITIONS

All books complete and unabridged. All 5³⁄₁₆" x 8¹⁄₄," paperbound.
Just $1.00–$2.00 in U.S.A.

A selection of the more than 200 titles in the series.

POETRY

DOVER · THRIFT · EDITIONS

All books complete and unabridged. All 5³⁄₁₆ x 8¼, paperbound.
Just $1.00—$2.00 in U.S.A.

GREAT LOVE POEMS, Shane Weller (ed.). 128pp. 27284-2 $1.00
SELECTED POEMS, Walt Whitman. 128pp. 26878-0 $1.00
THE BALLAD OF READING GAOL AND OTHER POEMS, Oscar Wilde. 64pp. 27072-6 $1.00
FAVORITE POEMS, William Wordsworth. 80pp. 27073-4 $1.00
EARLY POEMS, William Butler Yeats. 128pp. 27808-5 $1.00

FICTION

FLATLAND: A ROMANCE OF MANY DIMENSIONS, Edwin A. Abbott. 96pp. 27263-X $1.00
PERSUASION, Jane Austen. 224pp. 29555-9 $2.00
PRIDE AND PREJUDICE, Jane Austen. 272pp. 28473-5 $2.00
SENSE AND SENSIBILITY, Jane Austen. 272pp. 29049-2 $2.00
BEOWULF, Beowulf (trans. by R. K. Gordon). 64pp. 27264-8 $1.00
CIVIL WAR STORIES, Ambrose Bierce. 128pp. 28038-1 $1.00
TARZAN OF THE APES, Edgar Rice Burroughs. 224pp. 29570-2 $2.00
ALICE'S ADVENTURES IN WONDERLAND, Lewis Carroll. 96pp. 27543-4 $1.00
O PIONEERS!, Willa Cather. 128pp. 27785-2 $1.00
FIVE GREAT SHORT STORIES, Anton Chekhov. 96pp. 26463-7 $1.00
FAVORITE FATHER BROWN STORIES, G. K. Chesterton. 96pp. 27545-0 $1.00
THE AWAKENING, Kate Chopin. 128pp. 27786-0 $1.00
HEART OF DARKNESS, Joseph Conrad. 80pp. 26464-5 $1.00
THE SECRET SHARER AND OTHER STORIES, Joseph Conrad. 128pp. 27546-9 $1.00
THE "LITTLE REGIMENT" AND OTHER CIVIL WAR STORIES, Stephen Crane. 80pp. 29557-5 $1.00
THE OPEN BOAT AND OTHER STORIES, Stephen Crane. 128pp. 27547-7 $1.00
THE RED BADGE OF COURAGE, Stephen Crane. 112pp. 26465-3 $1.00
A CHRISTMAS CAROL, Charles Dickens. 80pp. 26865-9 $1.00
THE CRICKET ON THE HEARTH AND OTHER CHRISTMAS STORIES, Charles Dickens. 128pp. 28039-X $1.00
THE DOUBLE, Fyodor Dostoyevsky. 128pp. 29572-9 $1.50
NOTES FROM THE UNDERGROUND, Fyodor Dostoyevsky. 96pp. 27053-X $1.00
THE ADVENTURE OF THE DANCING MEN AND OTHER STORIES, Sir Arthur Conan Doyle. 80pp. 29558-3 $1.00
SIX GREAT SHERLOCK HOLMES STORIES, Sir Arthur Conan Doyle. 112pp. 27055-6 $1.00
SILAS MARNER, George Eliot. 160pp. 29246-0 $1.50
MADAME BOVARY, Gustave Flaubert. 256pp. 29257-6 $2.00
WHERE ANGELS FEAR TO TREAD, E. M. Forster. 128pp. (Available in U.S. only) 27791-7 $1.00
THE OVERCOAT AND OTHER STORIES, Nikolai Gogol. 112pp. 27057-2 $1.00
GREAT GHOST STORIES, John Grafton (ed.). 112pp. 27270-2 $1.00
THE MABINOGION, Lady Charlotte E. Guest. 192pp. 29541-9 $2.00
THE LUCK OF ROARING CAMP AND OTHER STORIES, Bret Harte. 96pp. 27271-0 $1.00
THE SCARLET LETTER, Nathaniel Hawthorne. 192pp. 28048-9 $2.00
YOUNG GOODMAN BROWN AND OTHER STORIES, Nathaniel Hawthorne. 128pp. 27060-2 $1.00
THE GIFT OF THE MAGI AND OTHER SHORT STORIES, O. Henry. 96pp. 27061-0 $1.00
THE NUTCRACKER AND THE GOLDEN POT, E. T. A. Hoffmann. 128pp. 27806-9 $1.00
THE BEAST IN THE JUNGLE AND OTHER STORIES, Henry James. 128pp. 27552-3 $1.00
THE TURN OF THE SCREW, Henry James. 96pp. 26684-2 $1.00

DOVER · THRIFT · EDITIONS

All books complete and unabridged. All 5³/₁₆ x 8¹/₄, paperbound.
Just $1.00—$2.00 in U.S.A.

DUBLINERS, James Joyce. 160pp. 26870-5 $1.00

A PORTRAIT OF THE ARTIST AS A YOUNG MAN, James Joyce. 192pp. 28050-0 $2.00

THE MAN WHO WOULD BE KING AND OTHER STORIES, Rudyard Kipling. 128pp. 28051-9 $1.00

SELECTED SHORT STORIES, D. H. Lawrence. 128pp. 27794-1 $1.00

GREEN TEA AND OTHER GHOST STORIES, J. Sheridan LeFanu. 96pp. 27795-X $1.00

THE CALL OF THE WILD, Jack London. 64pp. 26472-6 $1.00

FIVE GREAT SHORT STORIES, Jack London. 96pp. 27063-7 $1.00

WHITE FANG, Jack London. 160pp. 26968-X $1.00

THE NECKLACE AND OTHER SHORT STORIES, Guy de Maupassant. 128pp. 27064-5 $1.00

BARTLEBY AND BENITO CERENO, Herman Melville. 112pp. 26473-4 $1.00

THE GOLD-BUG AND OTHER TALES, Edgar Allan Poe. 128pp. 26875-6 $1.00

TALES OF TERROR AND DETECTION, Edgar Allan Poe. 96pp. 28744-0 $1.00

THE QUEEN OF SPADES AND OTHER STORIES, Alexander Pushkin. 128pp. 28054-3 $1.00

FRANKENSTEIN, Mary Shelley. 176pp. 28211-2 $1.00

THREE LIVES, Gertrude Stein. 176pp. 28059-4 $2.00

THE STRANGE CASE OF DR. JEKYLL AND MR. HYDE, Robert Louis Stevenson. 64pp. 26688-5 $1.00

TREASURE ISLAND, Robert Louis Stevenson. 160pp. 27559-0 $1.00

GULLIVER'S TRAVELS, Jonathan Swift. 240pp. 29273-8 $2.00

THE KREUTZER SONATA AND OTHER SHORT STORIES, Leo Tolstoy. 144pp. 27805-0 $1.00

ADVENTURES OF HUCKLEBERRY FINN, Mark Twain. 224pp. 28061-6 $2.00

THE MYSTERIOUS STRANGER AND OTHER STORIES, Mark Twain. 128pp. 27069-6 $1.00

CANDIDE, Voltaire (François-Marie Arouet). 112pp. 26689-3 $1.00

"THE COUNTRY OF THE BLIND" AND OTHER SCIENCE-FICTION STORIES, H. G. Wells. 160pp. (Available in U.S. only) 29569-9 $1.50

THE INVISIBLE MAN, H. G. Wells. 112pp. (Available in U.S. only) 27071-8 $1.00

THE WAR OF THE WORLDS, H. G. Wells. 160pp. (Available in U.S. only) 29506-0 $1.00

ETHAN FROME, Edith Wharton. 96pp. 26690-7 $1.00

THE PICTURE OF DORIAN GRAY, Oscar Wilde. 192pp. 27807-7 $1.00

MONDAY OR TUESDAY: Eight Stories, Virginia Woolf. 64pp. 29453-6 $1.00

NONFICTION

THE DEVIL'S DICTIONARY, Ambrose Bierce. 144pp. 27542-6 $1.00

THE SOULS OF BLACK FOLK, W. E. B. Du Bois. 176pp. 28041-1 $2.00

SELF-RELIANCE AND OTHER ESSAYS, Ralph Waldo Emerson. 128pp. 27790-9 $1.00

THE AUTOBIOGRAPHY OF BENJAMIN FRANKLIN, Benjamin Franklin. 144pp. 29073-5 $1.50

THE STORY OF MY LIFE, Helen Keller. 80pp. 29249-5 $1.00

GREAT SPEECHES, Abraham Lincoln. 112pp. 26872-1 $1.00

THE PRINCE, Niccolò Machiavelli. 80pp. 27274-5 $1.00

SYMPOSIUM AND PHAEDRUS, Plato. 96pp. 27798-4 $1.00

THE TRIAL AND DEATH OF SOCRATES: Four Dialogues, Plato. 128pp. 27066-1 $1.00

CIVIL DISOBEDIENCE AND OTHER ESSAYS, Henry David Thoreau. 96pp. 27563-9 $1.00

THE THEORY OF THE LEISURE CLASS, Thorstein Veblen. 256pp. 28062-4 $2.00

DOVER · THRIFT · EDITIONS

All books complete and unabridged. All 5³⁄₁₆" x 8¹⁄₄," paperbound.
Just $1.00–$2.00 in U.S.A.

PLAYS

PROMETHEUS BOUND, Aeschylus. 64pp. 28762-9 $1.00

WHAT EVERY WOMAN KNOWS, James Barrie. 80pp. (Available in U.S. only) 29578-8 $1.50

THE CHERRY ORCHARD, Anton Chekhov. 64pp. 26682-6 $1.00

THE THREE SISTERS, Anton Chekhov. 64pp. 27544-2 $1.00

THE WAY OF THE WORLD, William Congreve. 80pp. 27787-9 $1.50

BACCHAE, Euripides. 64pp. 29580-X $1.00

MEDEA, Euripides. 64pp. 27548-5 $1.00

THE MIKADO, William Schwenck Gilbert. 64pp. 27268-0 $1.00

FAUST, PART ONE, Johann Wolfgang von Goethe. 192pp. 28046-2 $2.00

SHE STOOPS TO CONQUER, Oliver Goldsmith. 80pp. 26867-5 $1.50

A DOLL'S HOUSE, Henrik Ibsen. 80pp. 27062-9 $1.00

HEDDA GABLER, Henrik Ibsen. 80pp. 26469-6 $1.00

VOLPONE, Ben Jonson. 112pp. 28049-7 $1.50

DR. FAUSTUS, Christopher Marlowe. 64pp. 28208-2 $1.00

THE MISANTHROPE, Molière. 64pp. 27065-3 $1.00

THE EMPEROR JONES, Eugene O'Neill. 64pp. 29268-1 $1.50

RIGHT YOU ARE, IF YOU THINK YOU ARE, Luigi Pirandello. 64pp. (Available in U.S. only) 29576-1 $1.50

HANDS AROUND, Arthur Schnitzler. 64pp. 28724-6 $1.00

HAMLET, William Shakespeare. 128pp. 27278-8 $1.00

HENRY IV, William Shakespeare. 96pp. 29584-2 $1.00

JULIUS CAESAR, William Shakespeare. 80pp. 26876-4 $1.00

KING LEAR, William Shakespeare. 112pp. 28058-6 $1.00

MACBETH, William Shakespeare. 96pp. 27802-6 $1.00

A MIDSUMMER NIGHT'S DREAM, William Shakespeare. 80pp. 27067-X $1.00

ROMEO AND JULIET, William Shakespeare. 96pp. 27557-4 $1.00

ARMS AND THE MAN, George Bernard Shaw. 80pp. (Available in U.S. only) 26476-9 $1.50

THE SCHOOL FOR SCANDAL, Richard Brinsley Sheridan. 96pp. 26687-7 $1.00

ANTIGONE, Sophocles. 64pp. 27804-2 $1.00

OEDIPUS REX, Sophocles. 64pp. 26877-2 $1.00

MISS JULIE, August Strindberg. 64pp. 27281-8 $1.50

THE PLAYBOY OF THE WESTERN WORLD AND RIDERS TO THE SEA, J. M. Synge. 80pp. 27562-0 $1.50

THE IMPORTANCE OF BEING EARNEST, Oscar Wilde. 64pp. 26478-5 $1.00

For a complete descriptive list of all volumes in the Dover Thrift Editions series
write for a free Dover Fiction and Literature Catalog (59047-X) to
Dover Publications, Inc., Dept. DTE, 31 E. 2nd Street, Mineola, N.Y. 11501